Nocturne

BY

Elizabeth Ellen Carter

with bonus story

SEPTEMBER HARVEST

NOCTURNE
© Elizabeth Ellen Carter, 2016
First published 2016
SEPTEMBER HARVEST
© Elizabeth Ellen Carter, 2018
First published 2015
www.eecarter.com
Published by Business Communications Management

Cover Illustrations / Photographs by
The Killion Group, Inc (Regency Couple); vige.co | dollarphotoclub.com (Old Paper Texture); boxoffrogs | dollarphotoclub.com (Piano 3)
September Harvest title illustration by Ingram Image

Cover Design and Print Edition Formatting by
Business Communications Management | bcm-online.com.au

Nocturne
Carter, Elizabeth Ellen
ISBN 978-0-6483852-1-9

CONTENTS

ACKNOWLEDGEMENTS

Thank you is such an inadequate expression of gratitude
to my darling husband who edits and designs tirelessly,
and inspires constantly.

Thank you also to Susanne Bellamy
for her feedback and encouragement.

Nocturne

Music should strike fire from the heart of man,
and bring tears from the eyes of woman.

– Ludwig van Beethoven

Chapter One

The unsealed letter shook in Ella Montgomery's hand but it was as much from the jostling of the rough road and gusting wind outside as it was from her shivering with cold inside the frigid carriage.

An icy blast hit the vehicle broadside, rocking it on its axles. The horses whinnied in distress.

"Whoa there."

Outside, the driver drew the beasts to a halt and climbed down, calling out to Ella, "Won't be long, miss, just calmin' the 'orses." A minute later the coach lurched as the man climbed back to his seat. Ella heard the snap of the reins over the howling wind. The carriage jolted into motion again.

The light had nearly gone from this dismal afternoon, hidden behind unyielding steel grey clouds threatening to drop more snow. It was too cold to open the curtains that, at least, kept out the wind, and it seemed too much of a waste to light the lamp to read by.

Ella carefully refolded the letter and returned it to her muff. She didn't need to see it again anyway – she knew it already by heart.

It was a letter of personal recommendation from Bishop Stanton lamenting the loss of the Reverend Matthew Montgomery. He attested to Reverend Montgomery's good character and, by extension, his daughter's own disposition. The second page was a list of Ella's accomplishments – English and French, painting, embroidery and music.

The Bishop had described her as a plain but honest young woman who would be unfailing in her duties.

Ella smiled in wistful remembrance. *Dear Papa*. Her father died disappointed she remained unwed in his lifetime – not for his sake, but for hers.

"You're a fine girl who only wants to be rid of shyness," he had insisted on more than one occasion, but Ella was convinced the Bishop's description of her as plain was more accurate. Her face was too thin, her hair too mousy – there were twenty other girls in their village prettier than her by far.

At twenty-four, she was older than most new governesses but the death of her father had left her with no choice but to go into service. Her only advantage was an education, which she was now to share with two little girls. Grace and Louisa Worsley were five-year-old twins and that's all she knew of her charges.

Blackheath Manor was her first posting.

The carriage slowed to a halt once more and, with a squeak of rain-soaked wood, a little hatch opened at the front. Cold air rushed in along with the words of the driver.

"We be turnin' in't Black'eaf Manor now, miss."

The hatch closed around a swirl of icy mist before she could give her thanks.

Ella reached a black gloved hand to the heavy curtains of the door window for a first glimpse of her new home.

There was little she could see of it looming out of the fog. The grounds wore a mantle of snow. The trees, that in summer would spread their leafy canopy wide, were bare; skeletal arms rose heavenward supplicating for the end of the dreary weather.

Through a break in the miasma, the spire of the village church with its crown of snow rose out of the dale and stood proud. There was supposed to be a village nearby, but it remained out of view. Ella felt as though she was in the middle of nowhere. A prickle of loneliness struck her anew.

She breathed in deeply, filling her lungs with cold winter air and readied herself as the carriage rolled to a halt for a final time. Feeling the coach rock as the driver climbed down, she buttoned up her coat and wrapped the thick black woolen scarf that was her father's around her neck several times. The door opened and she accepted the assistance of the coachman onto the ground.

The facade of Blackheath Manor was just as austere as the weather; not even its deep red brick offered any warmth. The broad stone steps swept up to heavy oak doors that remained resolutely closed. Ella quieted a whole garden of butterflies flapping their wings in her stomach.

She threaded her gloved fingers into the warmth of the old woolen muff and followed the coachman hauling her meager baggage – a single small trunk and a leather hold-all – up the stairs and to the footman who finally opened the door to them.

"Wevvers no good for travellin'," the coachman grumbled, dropping Ella's baggage at the man's feet.

"Go round to the back of the house; cook'll have something for you there," the footman told him. The driver turned and descended the stairs with scarcely another glance at Ella.

The footman dragged her trunk and bag indoors, stood aside for her to step in and shut the door. "Wait here, miss," he said, looking her up and down, and left.

When he had gone, the silence was deafening. The banshee howl of the wind outside barely penetrated the walls of Blackheath Manor; the loudest noise was the metronome-like ticking of the long-case clock across the room, hypnotic in its regularity.

Ella stood alone in the dark oak paneled space of the grand entrance hall. Brass lanterns resembling gilded birdcages hung from the ceiling. In each cage, three oil lamps glowed.

Illuminated by the dim overhead lanterns and what weak light filtered in from outside through the tall sash windows, generations of the Worsley family stared at her implacably from their portraits on the walls.

She felt inferior under the dead gaze of these proud men and beautiful bejeweled women dressed in the styles of by-gone times. Brass plaques on the frames beneath each one made the introductions.

William Worsley, the first Earl of Renthorpe, dressed in the style of Charles II with his long, curly black hair spilling over his shoulders, watched her coldly.

At least the large fire in the ancient stone hearth at the end of the room offered some warmth, she thought as she approached it. The light was also better here and Ella examined the last three portraits.

The first, a man with dark hair and close-cropped beard, his hand on the head of a large hunting dog, struck a conceited pose. The brass plaque identified him as William Worsley V, the current Earl.

Next was a portrait of a striking young woman with light brown hair. She was dressed in a powder blue riding habit in the latest fashion with military-style epaulettes and gold frogging on the coat.

Ella turned her back to the fire momentarily and allowed its golden glow to warm her further before returning her attention to the portraits.

The last was of two young men, about the same age as the Earl. The first thing to strike her was how much they looked like one another. But perhaps it was an illusion caused by the fact that both men wore uniforms – their jackets scarlet with blue-green facing.

The family resemblance between the Earl and the officers was unmistakable, yet there were differences between them. The Earl's expression was austere while the artist had caught a hint of merriment and good-natured mischief in the faces of the two men in uniform.

The more Ella looked, the more she was drawn to the man on the left. The engraved plaque on the frame informed her this was Thomas Worsley. His rich brown eyes seemed to look at her directly and the longer she gazed, the deeper they seemed to draw her in. Her heart beat time with the crisp tick-tick of the clock – the only sound she could hear anywhere in the house, she realized.

The first three gongs sounded to mark the hour.

"We expected you at lunch, Miss Montgomery."

Ella started at the disapproving words and pivoted to face a woman dressed head-to-toe in black.

Chapter Two

"**F**orgive me," Ella rushed out breathlessly, her heart now beating a triple meter. "The snow made the journey slow."

Her explanation did little to impress the heavy set middle-aged woman before her.

"Well, I can offer you no hot food until supper," she warned, making no attempt to disguise her censure. "I shall have a maid bring a cold plate to your room. At five o'clock you may meet your charges and arrange their evening meal and bath. Be ready at seven o'clock to be introduced to the master and mistress in the drawing room."

Ella blinked at the rapid fire instructions, still no wiser as to the woman's identity but, judging by the plain severity of her long sleeved gown, relieved by the edge of lace on the neck and cuffs and a glint of silver from the collection of keys at her waist, suspected she must be the housekeeper.

Behind her as she spoke, the footman slipped into the room, hefted Ella's trunk and bag, and left just as noiselessly.

Ella's eyes flicked from him back to the woman as she continued, "Addie will show you to your room."

From a door by the fireplace that Ella hadn't noticed, a young maid emerged. She bobbed her head to the housekeeper and then dropped a small curtsy to Ella.

The older woman moved off toward the service passage, and then paused as though she had recalled something forgotten.

"You may call me Mrs. Mellor."

The sound of the woman's sharp footsteps echoing down to a basement floor competed with the crackle of the fire and the sound of the clock.

This was not the greeting Ella had expected all the way from Lincolnshire, although she wasn't sure what sort of reception she might receive. Perhaps the master and mistress of the house would greet her with a smile and introduce their two delightful daughters who might have a posy of flowers waiting for her...

The warm welcoming scene played itself out in her head as little red-headed Addie led her out of the entrance hall back into the foyer. To the left, she was informed, was the drawing room. They climbed the dark oak stairs to the first landing. Addie opened the first door to the right.

It was a large room painted white. The tall windows let in plenty of light – grey and soft with the falling snow. Addie closed the door as she left and Ella was alone once more.

She listened for the sound of children and heard none, yet there was evidence of their presence. Two desks sat side-by-side facing a chalkboard. Near the window were two child-sized embroidery loops and a wicker basket, no doubt containing multi-hued silks.

Various cupboards and bookcases filled with children's books lined the wall closest to the door. It was the only bright spot in this poor benighted place. To Ella's left, along the short wall, another door was ajar and through it, she could see the edge of her trunk.

Her booted steps echoed on the timber floor until they were muted by the blue rag rug beside the bed. It was a single brass bed covered by a faded patchwork quilt. A pot cupboard beside the bed, a small wardrobe and a dressing table completed the furnishings. A small quantity of coals glowed red in the hearth but they barely took the chill off the room.

Ella crossed to the small window and looked out over the dales where she caught a glimpse of the village through the grove of trees and farmlands beyond, all wearing a blanket of snow.

Turning back to the room, Ella unpacked her precious few belongings. Before hanging them in the wardrobe, she laid her dresses on the bed to smooth them out – a winter Sunday dress of felt, the color of ripe raspberries, a forest green walking dress, and a Sunday dress for summer in soft buttery yellow linen, along with her slate grey day dress. The first three were all gifts from the Bishop's wife. They were hand-me-downs, but still of the finest quality and not too out of fashion.

As she hung the dresses up, she reflected that Mrs. Stanton's generosity had more than doubled her wardrobe. Before that she had owned only the grey day dress in addition to the black one she wore now.

Ella placed her most valued possession on the bed – her father's Bible. She stroked the black leather cover, rubbed soft with age, and opened it. Inside were her father's commentaries. Seeing his handwriting made her feel as though he were alive once more. Ella closed her eyes. The sharpness of his loss had barely lessened over the year.

She had never felt more miserable in her life.

The chimes from the grandfather clock echoed up the stairwell, registering the fourth hour of the afternoon. No one had yet brought the promised meal to her room – not that she was hungry, anyway.

She straightened her back, suddenly struck with the resolve to at least do something.

Although Mrs. Mellor had set a timetable, Ella was the girls' governess, and therefore they were her responsibility. She would see them now and introduce herself before they were to be presented to their parents at bedtime.

Ella took a tentative step or two toward the staircase and looked up to the top floor. She could hear no sounds there. If she listened hard, she could hear maids downstairs preparing the dining table. Then she looked to the left and the right. If the school room was on this floor, perhaps the nursery was as well.

She knocked on several closed doors and received no response. The house was a jumble of passages and Ella soon found herself at the last door before a narrow stone spiral staircase. The sounds of kitchen activity below confirmed her belief these were the servants' stairs.

She heard movement from behind the door – the scrape of a chair and a softly grunted curse. A moment's indecision, then her hand was raised to knock on the door when Mrs. Mellor startled her for the second time today.

"Are you looking for something, Miss Montgomery?" she asked sharply.

Ella turned and found the woman's expression as cold as the day outside.

"I'm seeking the nursery, Mrs. Mellor."

"You won't find it here."

"Then if you would kindly direct me—"

"On the second floor. It is the room above yours. Use the main staircase, not the servants'. You do not want to give the wrong impression when you are new here."

Mrs. Mellor extended her arms, drawing attention to a tray of food which Ella, so focused on Mrs. Mellor's stern expression, had not noticed. The tray bore an elaborate silver savory dish warmed underneath by two small votive candles. Beside it was a platter of fresh fruit, a wedge of cheese and a sweetmeat dish filled with nuts.

"Oh," said Ella, "I hope you didn't go to too much trouble on my account."

The woman frowned a moment, then saw Ella's gaze upon the tray and her look became glacial.

"This is not for you. I have more important duties than to be scullery maid to a governess. Get out of my way."

Mrs. Mellor set the tray on a side table opposite the door on which Ella had been about to knock. With cheeks flushed red, Ella turned and hurried back down the passageway. Behind her as she fled, she heard a male voice answer Mrs. Mellor's authoritative knock on the door.

Ella found the main stairs and started climbing, mentally berating herself. She had been here a scant two hours and gotten off on the wrong foot with one of the most important people in the house.

Her first post had not started well – and she had a horrible feeling it was not going to get any better.

Chapter Three

The door swung wide at Ella's first tentative tap and yet, at first glance, the room seemed uninhabited. Then two pretty dolls with long dark hair and matching but differently colored dresses stood up from the window seat and ran towards her.

"Are you our governess?" asked one, excitedly.

"Her name is Miss Montgomery," stated the other.

"I know that," replied the first.

Ella was immediately charmed.

"Remember what your maman says, you must be good girls."

The mild admonishment was given by an elderly woman who stepped from behind the door and gave Ella the first smile she had received since arriving at Blackheath Manor.

The woman introduced herself as Hester Proud. "And this is Grace and Louisa," she said.

"Which is which?" Ella asked, looking at the two children.

The girls looked at each other mischievously for a moment, but dropped their guile at a warning cough from the elderly woman.

"Louisa likes pink and Grace prefers yellow," she said.

And clothing is very easy for twins to swap, Ella thought to herself.

She dropped down to their level so she could look at them clearly. The resemblance between the girls was remarkable. She had never before seen identical twins, yet today she had seen two pairs – these girls and, seemingly, the two men in the portrait in the entrance hall.

Ella held out her hand and the girl in pink took it and bobbed a curtsy.

"How do you do? My name is Louisa."

Up close, Ella saw the girl had a faint smattering of freckles across her nose. She turned to Grace who introduced herself as her sister did, with a polite handshake and a curtsy. And she did not have the freckles.

There it was – a way to tell them apart to avoid any trickery.

"Remember girls," said the older woman, "you're going to be presented to your mama and papa tonight, so finish your drawings."

Louisa and Grace skipped off, hand in hand, to the far end of the nursery and settled at the table by the window.

"I was their mother's nanny," the woman explained, smiling at the girls who were engrossed in their tasks. Grace's tongue crept out of the corner of her mouth as she concentrated on her picture.

"Louisa and Gracie are delightful girls," she continued, "but I'm afraid I'm too old to keep up with them now. The world is changing and the girls need an education."

"You're staying on aren't you, Miss Proud?" Ella enquired.

"Do call me Hester... but no. I shall be leaving in the summer, as soon as the master and mistress are satisfied you've settled in. I have a sister in Harrogate, so I'll live with her."

Ella followed Hester and assisted as she tidied the nursery and put away clothes in the girls' shared bedroom. Twin beds, one with a coverlet in pink and the other in yellow, made this by far the cheeriest room in Blackheath Manor that Ella had seen.

She listened as the nanny shared her observations of her two charges – they were at their most active in the mornings and apt to lose concentration mid-afternoon, when a nap was recommended for them. The girls did not like their vegetables and Mrs. Mellor would complain if food was wasted.

Ella was pleased to have successfully disguised an uncharitable reaction of distaste at the housekeeper's name.

"Do the girls play music?"

"There's been no one to teach them, which is a great shame. The current mistress's mother, Millicent, had an endowment, but alas her daughter inherited the piano and the harp but not the talent."

By the time the grandfather clock struck the seventh hour, it was black night outside. Louisa and Grace made their way down the grand staircase one careful step at a time in their matching long nightgowns with Ella between them, holding their hands. Hester followed behind with their portfolio of pictures.

Ella willed the nervous effervescence in her stomach to settle as they approached the closed drawing room door. Once there, she let go of the girls' hands to sweep away loose strands of hair from her face and accept the portfolio of pictures proffered by Hester. As the nanny knocked on the door, Louisa and Grace clasped each other's hand.

"Enter."

It sounded like the voice of the man in the room on the first floor.

Hester opened the door and she and Ella allowed the children to walk into the drawing room before them.

Here were the children's parents. Their mother, seated by the fire, went almost unnoticed by Ella at first. Her eye was drawn to their father. Instead of a hunting dog, a table with a decanter of claret atop stood beside him. Behind him was the piano Hester had mentioned. Ella's first thought was the artist had caught his likeness well, right down to the thin line of his mouth.

She curtsied to the Earl of Renthorpe and introduced herself.

"Miss Montgomery," he replied in a disinterested tone.

She drew her eyes away from him to take in the drawing room which was magnificent and tastefully furnished in the very latest fashion. Wallpaper of sprigged flowers and serpentine stripe in sky blue decorated the walls. Almost hidden behind a pillar was the harp.

Ella remembered herself and curtsied to the children's mother.

Lady Margaret resembled her daughters in looks with the shape of her face and fine porcelain skin. Ella had thought the look on her face rather dull as they entered the room, but the woman's expression lifted at her daughters' arrival.

As for the girls themselves, they dutifully curtsied to their father and wished him a good evening before turning to their mother to give the same rote greeting.

"Lady Louisa, Lady Grace," said Ella, using the girls' formal titles, "will you show your mother and father what you have done today?"

Louisa and Grace accepted the portfolio from Ella's hands. The room descended into an awkward silence as the girls looked from one parent to another for any hint of encouragement. Eventually Lady Margaret reached out her hand.

"Show them to me, girls."

"This is Sooty the cat. See? She's asleep by the hearth."

"That's very good, Louisa."

"Mama, I drew a picture of papa on his horse."

Margaret dutifully examined Grace's picture and praised it.

"William, take a look at the fine work your daughters have done."

The Earl put down his glass of claret – reluctantly in Ella's opinion – and took the drawings from his wife's hands.

The girls watched their father keenly, waiting for kind and encouraging words, Ella supposed. Instead, his first comment was to her.

"Are these satisfactory, Miss Montgomery?"

Ella's heart broke. Two small girls wanted this man's approval so much and it seemed that little kindness was to be denied them.

"Considering they are only five-years-old and have had no training," Ella replied as mildly as she could, "I would say Lady Louisa and Lady Grace show promise."

"I think both my girls have done very well," said Lady Margaret and she bestowed a smile on each child. "Give maman a hug before bed."

The Earl's mouth thinned further.

"Oh, for God's sake Margaret! You'll ruin your gown even before our guests arrive."

There was no mistaking the look of contempt Lady Margaret gave her husband in response. Almost in defiance it seemed, the woman straightened on the wingback chair and opened her arms wide, accepting the children's enthusiastic embrace.

"All right, girls," announced Hester. "Wish the Earl and Countess good night."

"Good night, papa. God bless you. Good night, mama. God bless you," said Louisa and Grace in sing-song unison.

Ella turned aside and waited for the girls, who held hands once again, to file past her to Hester's guiding hand. She went to follow the girls, eager, in fact, to escape the coldness in the room.

"Miss Montgomery. A word with you."

She paused and turned back to her employers. Behind her the door clicked shut. The Earl looked her up and down.

She had felt inferior to the portraits in the hall. Now, already, Ella could tell she had been found wanting in the flesh.

Chapter Four

Oh papa, why did you have to die and leave me by myself? Oh Father in Heaven, I don't know if I can do this alone.

Ella huddled beneath the inadequate blankets in the inadequately heated room. The overcoat she'd thrown across the covers had made only a marginal difference. The salt from her tears made her face feel rough and tight.

The interview with the Earl had not gone well. She would be ordered to have her bags packed again tomorrow, she was certain...

"Now you have met Grace and Louisa, do you feel adequately prepared to discharge your duties?" he had asked.

"Yes, sir. Your daughters are bright and engaged little girls, they will be a delight to teach, I'm sure."

Their father had grunted, though whether in approval of her answer or not, Ella couldn't be certain.

"Where are your lesson plans?"

"Sir? But I only arrived this afternoon..." Ella knew instantly her answer displeased him, and she attempted to explain further. "I have broad plans, of course, but I couldn't develop lessons until I had met my pupils, discovered their aptitudes and interests, and—"

"I don't particularly care what you claim you can or cannot do—"

It was the Earl's turn to be interrupted in mid-sentence.

"William..." his wife reproved, but he acknowledged her with only a quick glance of disdain and she said nothing more in Ella's defense as he continued addressing her.

"I am paying you to teach, Montgomery, not have a holiday at my expense."

Ella became conscious of her mouth being open. She closed it and swallowed past the rising lump in her throat. The terms of her employment were far from extravagant. She was to have room and board plus thirty pounds a year, a half day off on Sundays and a full day one Wednesday each month.

"You have a month to prove your worth," the Earl continued. "And I want to see improvement in the children by the end of the next week."

With that, she had been brusquely dismissed to her supper, which she ate with little relish despite her hunger...

Ella now rubbed her nose and burrowed further under the blankets. Tears sprang to her eyes once more as she thought about her dear gentle father. The man loved her dearly and was always there with a ready smile and to indulge her insatiable thirst for knowledge.

They had rambled over the dales and he would show her the most wonderful things. Roman ruins and remains of Anglo Saxon forts. He taught her the names of wild flowers in the meadow. He even showed her how to fish. More than that, he loved her and was never afraid to show it. The Reverend Montgomery was the most compassionate man she had known, unstinting in devotion to his flock, especially the children.

"Remember the words of Christ," he once reminded her. "*Take heed that ye despise not one of these little ones; for I say unto you, that in heaven their angels do always behold the face of my Father which is in heaven.*"

Ella wished the Earl would remember those words; he had surely once been taught them. Quietly, she said a prayer for the Worsley family – a custom she had started under the many roofs she had stayed beneath in the time since her father's death.

The prayer for others steadied her too and, after a few moments, Ella felt more calm.

Although it was many hours before the dawn, sleep fled. She had only a week to win the Earl's favor. That meant discovering how much the girls already knew of reading, writing and arithmetic, and improving on it. She was confident the twins would be attentive – even school work would be a welcome distraction from the dreary winter days.

Ella got up, slipped the overcoat over her faded flannel night gown, and used a taper in the dying coals of her small fireplace to relight her bedside candle. She opened the connecting door to the schoolroom and crossed to the fireplace in there.

She soon coaxed some flame for warmth from the low burning coals and lit an oil lamp for sufficient light to see and write at the table so she could extinguish her candle.

The first activity was the Earl's demanded lesson plan for his daughters. It was pride as much as fear that drove Ella to work past the midnight hour that chimed from the hallway below. She determined William Worsley, neither the portrait nor the man, would find her wanting in any way, shape or form.

When she had finished to her satisfaction, she went back to her room and retrieved her long neglected journal. Writing in it was a daily habit she had abandoned following her father's death, but now it seemed appropriate to address it once again.

Words flowed onto the page in Ella's neat cursive script. She shared with her mute companion the journey to Blackheath Manor, her encounter with Mrs. Mellor, her hopes for her charges, and of the tensions that seemed to dog this old house.

As Ella wrote, the low, constant noise of the wind outside and the loud ticking of the hall clock below grew less and less in her consciousness until the scratching of pen on paper seemed the loudest sound in the world.

A dull thunk from somewhere in the house started her from a half doze at the table.

She lifted the chimney on the lamp to light her candle before extinguishing the lamp. A warm satisfaction filled her in contrast to her earlier despair. Ella knew she would make a very good governess, even the Bishop thought so.

She would not let this place overwhelm her.

She settled back into her bed. Her lids closed of their own accord, heavy with fatigue.

In the last vestiges of conscious thought before sleep claimed her completely, Ella fancied she could hear the melody of a piano concerto and recognized it as a composition in E-flat major by Haydn. She smiled.

Her late mother loved music and had taught her to play, and her father had encouraged her to continue with it after her mother's death.

The imagined notes from a skilled player reminded her of happier times, a recital in the summer during her youth, perhaps.

Ella was deeply asleep long before the *adagio e cantabile* was even halfway through.

Chapter Five

Sunday dawned crisp and clear, the sky a pure aqua blue made all the brighter by streaks of pristine white clouds.

It had been five days since Ella had arrived at Blackheath Manor and today was the first time she had left its walls.

With Grace at her right and Louisa on her left, the girls guided her along the cleared path to the village church. Next to it was the graveyard. The headstones cast purple shadows across the crystalline snow. Ella was too far away to read any of the markers but she decided she would spend a little time exploring after the service.

At the entrance to the church, she gave Louisa and Grace's hands a little squeeze to remind them to stop and wait as their mother and father walked down the aisle. The couple were side-by-side but a foot apart, their manner correct but lacking emotion or consideration one to the other.

Ella wondered what kind of marriage the Worsleys had, then rebuked herself for the thought. It was none of her business to have any kind of curiosity about her employers' lives, let alone here at church on Sunday.

Ella and the girls followed and sat in the pews behind the Earl and his wife. Around the oak clad walls were names of the notable locals of Renthorpe who were memorialized in the church. The Worsley family featured prominently and Ella's eyes skimmed across the names until they fell on two engraved on a bright brass plaque not tarnished by many years, as the others had been.

Robert Adam Worsley 1790-1815
Thomas James Worsley 1790-1815

died in service to King and Country

The dates were exactly the same. Her eyes slid across to William Worsley who was facing the altar, his posture rigidly correct in the pew. Robert and Thomas, the two young men, handsome in their red dress uniforms in the portrait – they were twins, just like the girls, and must have been the Earl's younger brothers.

Another plaque affixed to the back of the pew in front of her bore the name of William Albert Worsley, the fourth earl, and the dates 1752-1815.

An inkling of sympathy grew in Ella's breast for Lord Renthorpe. It seemed he had lost his father and both his brothers in the same year. No wonder Blackheath Manor seemed in a never-ending state of mourning.

The Reverend, a tall man with thinning hair and aged in his forties, Ella guessed, stepped forward, his white vestments flowing behind him, greeting his most distinguished parishioners.

Ella heard the rest of the worshippers rising to their feet behind her as the organist played the opening strains of *To Be A Pilgrim*. She rose too, bringing Louisa and Grace to stand as well, then bent to help first one, then the other find the correct page in the hymnal.

Who would true valor see,
Let him come hither;
One here will constant be,
Come wind, come weather
There's no discouragement
Shall make him once relent
His first avowed intent
To be a pilgrim.

The familiar rituals of the Sunday service were second nature to Ella as a vicar's daughter, and she reveled in them, recalling the happy days when she would sit in her father's study and watch him prepare his sermon.

Later in church, she would listen as he illustrated his message using scripture from his well-loved Bible, the one now on Ella's dressing table which she read every night.

In church, she not only felt close to God but also to her father and her mother, rest their souls. Would that William and Margaret Worsley know such peace, she thought, if not for their own sakes but that of their daughters.

The service ended before noon with the rousing hymn *Now Thank We All Our God.* Many of the townsfolk lingered in the courtyard after the service, conversing with friends and neighbors, enjoying the sunshine and trying to avoid the occasional gust of wind that reminded them winter still had more than a month to go.

The Earl and his wife spoke to some of the residents, staying only long enough to make their way to the carriage that would take them, and Louisa and Grace too, away for the day.

Servants from the house clustered together in groups. Most of them would be looking forward to enjoying their afternoon of liberty. Ella recognized many of them but Mrs. Mellor was not among them.

Despite the fact the housekeeper's room was only across the passage from her own, Ella had seen very little of her, not that she had made any special attempt to seek her out. She still had to prove her worth to the Earl and so had thrown herself completely into her work. She was grateful her students had taken to their lessons well, and seemed to enjoy practicing letters on their slates every morning.

A group of servants from the house made their way along the church path and out towards the woods bounding the Manor lands. No one spoke to her as they passed. She reflected that only Hester had shown her any kindness. Now the nanny approached.

"The stable hands have set up a game of skittles in one of the horse stalls. Did you want to join us?"

Ella smiled but shook her head.

"I've been invited by the vicar and his wife to stay for tea," she said, brushing a strand of hair, dislodged by the wind, from her eyes. "Blackheath is still a mystery to me. I want to know more about this place."

"You should be careful what you wish for then."

Before Ella could ask Hester to explain herself, she had squeezed her hands and wished her a good day before joining the trail of people making their way back to Blackheath Manor.

A couple of hours later, Ella left the vicar and his wife, telling them of her plans to explore the church grounds. She started at the far end, the oldest part of the graveyard.

Here the headstones were so weathered as to be almost illegible. Next week, she would be back with paper and a soft pencil to get some rubbings. Perhaps she would bring the girls as part of an excursion.

A carrion crow cried and Ella watched his flight from one tree to another, suddenly aware she was no longer alone in the cemetery. She watched two figures, a man and a woman, both in black, coming through the lych-gate.

To her surprise, the woman was none other than Mrs. Mellor. The man with her was much taller than the housekeeper but she guided his steps, his arm caught in hers until they emerged from the shelter of the gate onto the path. His arm now slipped from hers.

Mrs. Mellor spoke to him in low tones, too soft for Ella to hear. Perhaps she had misjudged the woman. It seemed she was here on an act of charity, assisting an old and infirm parishioner.

A wide brimmed hat pulled low over the man's face meant Ella could discern nothing of his features at the distance and she retreated behind a yew tree from where she could watch but remain unobserved.

As they walked, she could see the man moved cautiously. Each step showed he favored his left leg over his right. The stick in his right hand swept in front of him seeming to hunt for obstacles that might trip him.

His shoulders were broad and straight. It dawned on Ella belatedly that the man was not elderly.

Mrs. Mellor and the man paused at a near new granite memorial, not yet dulled or eroded by the weather. Ella watched as the housekeeper slipped a hand inside her coat and drew forth a posy of snowdrops and evergreens, tied in a red bow. She bent down, placing the token at the foot of the obelisk before helping her companion who made a slow and awkward descent to kneel before the stone.

Ella watched the man rest one hand on the plinth and reach out to touch the lettering on the stone with the other. He bowed his head, though whether in prayer or from the exertion of kneeling, she could not be certain. He spent some time in that position while Mrs. Mellor stood beside him, a silent sentry.

Who was he? Mrs. Mellor's son? No one had mentioned him. And where would he live? Surely not alone?

The quality of the light changed as the sun lowered, casting a golden glow over the landscape. This seemed to be some kind of signal because Mrs. Mellor touched the man on the shoulder and helped him rise.

Stiffly at first, then with more ease as he accepted her arm again, he left the graveyard and walked with Mrs. Mellor towards the copse of trees that would lead them to the Manor.

Ella's curiosity was overwhelming. She waited until the housekeeper and the mysterious stranger disappeared into the shadows before heading straight for the memorial that had been their focus.

It was the Worsley family memorial and the inscription they had faced was similar to the plaque inside the church:

Robert Adam Worsley
Thomas James Worsley

Died with valor in the service of their King

1790-1815

Perhaps the lame man had served with the brothers. That would make sense and, she reasoned, he must also live locally, for if he were a guest at the Manor, why hadn't she seen him?

Chapter Six

Ella forgot about Mrs. Mellor and the man at the cemetery as she spent the next weeks drilling her pupils on the upcoming presentation for their father. The girls had evidently fulfilled his desire to show 'improvement' at the end of Ella's first week – that she was still under the roof of Blackheath Manor was evidence of it – but she had no idea what improvement he had expected to see. The Earl had not mentioned a thing since.

Now, she trained up each girl for the day they would recite a short poem, read a psalm and name all the animals on an illustrated story board in both English and French.

At first, the twins had been excited to learn something new, but as the weeks wore on and more time was spent recalling what they had learned, Louisa and Grace's attention wavered. A change of scenery was the best remedy.

When the weather was inclement, their exercise was limited to a promenade along the second floor gallery. When the weather cleared and the sun shone, however weakly, Ella took them for walks in the grounds.

Her favorite activity of all was lessons at the piano in the drawing room.

Ella had started to teach the girls music, but their progress so far would not impress their father though, perhaps, if she was kept on, the girls might be allowed to give a short recital three months hence when they should have skill enough to play simple nursery rhymes.

In a separate notebook, Ella wrote observations of her charges, as well as what they had learned that day. As she got to know the girls, she learned more about what set them apart. Louisa had a great curiosity about the world around her but was short of attention. Grace would settle herself into a task and go about it quietly, but needed to be coaxed to try anything new.

Ella reasoned that if the Worsleys decided to terminate her employment, at least the next governess would not have to start at the beginning with the twins.

Tonight, she followed her daily routine, the continuation of a pattern set on her very first day. She would attend to Louisa and Grace's supper, then see them bathed and dressed for bed before they were presented to their mother and father to say good night.

Not once had William or Margaret sought their children out, not even to tuck them into bed, Ella noted.

Her evenings were spent alone. She did not dine with the servants, nor with the family. It seemed it was a governess's lot to be betwixt and between these two layers of society in a grand house.

Supper was served to Ella in the schoolroom, but even so, as she was coming to realize, to be alone wasn't necessarily to be lonely. She cleaned the school room every night after supper and documented Grace and Louisa's progress before reading a passage from her father's Bible – tonight had been the story of Ruth – then, having put on her nightdress, she would write in her journal before bed.

She had just taken pen in hand when she heard a door close nearby and a series of thumping steps fading away as they moved down the passageway.

She ignored the sounds. Movement was common in the house as staff went from place to place undertaking their duties, though she'd not previously noticed such leaden paces.

Ella began committing her private thoughts to her journal, as if addressing her father. Though she had put one subject to the back of her mind while busy with the girls these past weeks, it now came to the forefront again.

> *You might think this a dreadful fancy of mine, father, but I still find myself believing there is a mystery that fills the walls of Blackheath Manor.*
>
> *Who was the mysterious man with Mrs. Mellor, who presented such a stark and tragic figure in the graveyard? What interest did Robert and Thomas Worsley's memorial have for him?*
>
> *Shall I ignore what is no business of mine? I think I know what your answer would be, if you were here to give me counsel. But, alas, left to my own devices and friendless here at Blackheath, I find myself further and further left to the whims of my own imagination – surely a dangerous state to be in.*

The house was now silent. Ella laid down her pen in the stand and, blotting the page, pondered the questions posed in her journal. Then, faintly at first, as though it had come from a fragment of her own memory, she heard the opening notes of Beethoven's *Piano Sonata No. 14.*

Every night since her first under this roof, Ella had fallen asleep to the sound of a piano, faint and far away.

She had given it no thought, dismissing it as piece of comfort conjured up by her mind to help her sleep.

Tonight, however, she was up later than previously, and here she was – wide awake and listening to music that was real, the *adagio sostenuto* haunting in its sparseness.

Ella rose from the school room desk, opened the door onto the landing and ventured to the top of the stairs. The music was coming from the drawing room downstairs. Step by step, she descended in the dark, drawn by the beautiful playing.

Oh, how she would love to accompany such a talent. This was one of her favorite pieces; it reminded her of midnight and a full moon, and the still small hours where heaven and earth seemed to touch.

Ella's fingers stretched of their own accord, mimicking the position of the keys, remembering her own painstaking lessons with Mr. Rodgers, a music teacher from a nearby boys' academy, who played the organ at her father's church.

She waited at the door and listened. The quiet passion of the German composer's work tugged at her heart and, before she was aware of it, the cold brass of the door knob was in her hand. Her fingers closed over the handle and turned it.

The latch opened with a soft click, barely heard over the sound of the sonata. Ella opened the door a crack. The drawing room was in complete darkness, not even a lamp was lit to illuminate the sheet music and yet whoever was at the piano played on, flawless in execution.

Surely this was not Lady Margaret. Hester had told her the lady of the house had not inherited her mother's talent, and this was a piece being performed by an accomplished pianist.

It was unlikely to be a servant. Then who?

Ella pushed the door open a little further to better hear.

The playing stopped and a masculine voice, rough and harsh, called out.

"Who's there?"

Ella ran back up the stairs, pulling the nightdress up to her knees to clear each step. She hurriedly closed the door to the school room, snatched up the still-burning lamp and darted for her bedroom.

The light of the lamp bounced and flickered in the glass chimney, giving the effect of ghosts leaping across the ceiling at her. She climbed into bed and pulled the covers up to her neck.

The sound of her panting was harsh in her ears. Minute after long minute passed. Ella's heart pounded violently as she waited for an equally violent pounding at her door.

It never came and finally she calmed enough to extinguish the lamp.

Ella lay with her eyes open and pre-dawn light outside changed her thin window curtains from black to grey before she succumbed to sleep.

Chapter Seven

"C-H-A-T, chat," said Grace, pointing to the grey tabby in the colorful farm yard scene Ella held. A grin spread across the child's face as she found each animal from her list, saying its name and spelling it correctly in French and English.

"Why do the French say *chat*, when we say cat?" asked Louisa.

"That's an excellent question."

"Well?" said the little girl, smiling as she pressed for a proper response. "There has to be an excellent answer."

Ella responded with a smile of her own. It was always Louisa with the difficult questions.

"Tomorrow I shall tell you about the Tower of Babel and how God caused everyone to speak different languages," promised Ella.

"Why would God do that?"

"It's a long story. It will have to wait for the morning."

Normally Ella would be more than happy to accommodate the little girl's curiosity, but six o'clock was approaching and the Earl and the Countess would be waiting in the drawing room for them.

Tonight was the night of the test to decide whether Ella stayed or left.

It was bad enough her stomach was full of butterflies on that account, without the added dread that William Worsley would challenge her for eavesdropping on his witching hour performance last night.

Not at all refreshed from her few hours sleep, Ella had decided the only person in the house the phantom pianist could be was the master of the house himself – although it did nothing to explain what he was doing playing Beethoven in the dark.

"Oh Grace!"

Ella turned to an exasperated Hester who was mopping spilled milk from the little girl's dress. At that moment, the first of six chimes rang announcing the hour.

Hester raised her head, giving Ella a rueful grimace.

"You go downstairs and delay. I'll bring both girls down with me in just a moment."

Ella picked up her notes and the art boards for the demonstration and mustered her confidence before she descended to the drawing room. She hoped the Earl would not be irritated by her arriving without the girls, but most of all she prayed he had not seen her last night or, if he had, that he had not recognized her in the dark.

Or if he did, she thought in desperation, perhaps despite his surly demeanor he was enough a gentleman to act so by making no reference to her nocturnal roaming.

After all, someone who could play as exquisitely as he did last night must have some of the finer qualities of character...

Ella pulled her rambling thoughts in order and was about to knock at the drawing room door when she heard his angry voice within the room. She pulled her hand back as if from a flame before it could make contact with the wood.

"It has to stop! I will no longer have him lurking about down here in the middle of the night."

Lady Margaret's reply was as sharp as Ella had ever heard her.

"You cannot throw him out of his home!" she protested, and the Earl's response was explosive.

"*My* home! Blackheath Manor is *my* home! I decide who lives in my house as I damn well please!"

"Be reasonable William," pleaded Lady Margaret, "where will he go?"

"His regiment can damn well look after him! He can go to London and live off the Chelsea Pension."

Ella cautioned herself. She should not be listening to this. It was a private matter of no concern to her at all. She should knock on the door to give the Earl and Countess time to compose themselves before their children arrived. She raised her hand again, but could not bring herself to strike the door after hearing Lady Margaret's next words.

"He's your brother and your responsibility."

Ella held her breath.

"As you always go to great pains to remind me," replied the Earl, bitterly. "Tell me, Margaret, which of them were you in love with? Which did you dream of when we were in bed together, when you decided to conceive twins?"

The percussive noise of a single slap made Ella jump. The silence that followed seemed almost as violent as the words that preceded it. Ella covered her mouth, breathless in the whirlwind of emotion that swirled about. Behind her, she heard Louise and Grace in unison, counting down each step in French.

Un, deux, trois, quatre, cinq...

The girls shouldn't hear this.

Ella knocked boldly. The silence in the room beyond continued for a moment, before the brusque instruction to enter.

She counted to two before opening the door. The scene in the drawing room was picture perfect. If she had not heard the argument with her own ears, she would not have believed anything had happened. The Earl stood beside the table with a glass of brandy in his hand. Lady Margaret sat in her favored position by the fire.

The only sign of any discord was the heightened color of the Countess's cheeks and the way she nervously rubbed one hand with the other. She had struck the blow and it had been so hard as to hurt her own fingers.

Ella looked to the Earl. If she was right, the evidence would be written on his cheek but it was concealed by his close beard.

Ella curtsied to them both, determined to hide any hint she may have overheard what just transpired.

"Earl Renthorpe, Countess, I am pleased to report your daughters have made excellent progress over this past month. Lady Louisa and Lady Grace have advanced in their reading and have now started French lessons.

"Their skills in writing are also showing improvement."

Ella held out two paper covered exercise books. The Earl seemed to show no interest. Ella offered them to the girl's mother who, after a moment's hesitation, accepted the books and held them in her lap.

Ella stood to one side while Louisa and Grace were shepherded in by Hester.

"Bon soir, papa. Bon soir, maman," they chorused, and the greeting was accompanied by a curtsy.

"Lady Louisa and Lady Grace would like to demonstrate a selection of things they have learned this month," said Ella, and she turned to the girls and held her breath, positioning the first story board to the front. It was the farmyard.

"Grace, would you like to go first?"

The little girl shook her head. Ella gave her a reassuring smile and nodded to Louisa who showed no such sign of nerves. Ella pointed to the horse.

"Horse. H-O-R-S-E. Horse. Cheval. C-H-A—"

Ella raised an eyebrow.

"C-H-*E*-V-A-L." Louisa corrected herself. She went on to name and spell her list of animals flawlessly. Emboldened by her sister's success, Grace successfully answered her challenge – a chicken, a cat, a plow and the stable.

"Now Lady Louisa will recite Psalm 134 and Lady Grace will recite Psalm 131, followed by a reading of–"

"I think that will be enough," said Earl Renthorpe.

His eyes met Ella's. She refused to let hers fall away.

Yes, it was a challenge, perhaps even defiance, but she did not care. The girls craved their father's approval and, no matter how remote both their parents were, Louisa and Grace did love them. Ella waited for the Earl to continue.

In the silent contest of wills, it was he who broke first.

"Louisa, Grace – you have both done well."

The girls beamed and it was all Ella could do to stop herself doing so as well.

Lady Margaret bade her daughters goodnight as did their father. Ella remained in place, waiting to be given her leave.

"I think you've proved your point, Miss Montgomery," said the Earl.

"Then you have found my work satisfactory, so far?"

"So far."

Ella accepted the man's gaze upon her without blinking. His expression remained neutral, giving no hint of his thoughts. The grandfather clock ticked off several seconds before he went on.

"You're excused."

Ella left with her head held high and, when her back was turned, allowed a victorious grin to emerge.

Chapter Eight

Ella kissed the girls good night. They were tired and, as their eyes closed, Ella whispered how proud she was of them both. She gave Hester a hug for good measure once the bedroom door had closed.

"Thank you. You have become my only ally here," she said.

The woman wiped away a small tear.

"No need for thanks. I'm just glad I can leave here for Yorkshire knowing those girls have someone to care for them and to love them."

"Oh they do, Hester, they most certainly do."

Ella hugged the woman once more.

"There's only one thing I ask," said Hester. "Have Louisa and Gracie practice their letters and remember their old nanny."

"Do you have your sister's address?" Ella enquired.

Hester shook her head. "But I shall write as soon as I arrive."

***

Ella skipped downstairs from the second floor nursery to the schoolroom. Readying herself for bed, she softly hummed the light and vibrant melody of Mozart's *Sonata No. 5* and sat to compose her journal entry.

Today was a victory, father. Oh how I wish you could have seen my charges. Never have I enjoyed a day more than today when Louisa and Grace performed so admirably for their mother and father.

The Earl even spared a word of praise for his daughters, which might show the man does not have a heart of stone despite all indications contrary wise.

Was that unkind of me? If I have to ask the question, then I know what the answer already is, so I repent for my uncharitable thinking.

Do I tell you your daughter is an eavesdropper? Being in heaven I'm sure you already know and are ashamed of me. I'm ashamed of myself but I cannot unhear what I have heard.

There is a brother who is not dead and the Earl believes his wife had a 'tendre' for one or perhaps both of them. Does this explain the Earl's remoteness towards Grace and Louisa? I shouldn't like to think so.

I am beginning to love both little girls dearly. I think I can be most happy here if my days were more like today than not.

Ella put down her pen. There was more she could write in her journal, but she was not ready to commit her thoughts even to the privacy of her book.

Who's there?

Clearly the voice was not William Worsley's.

Ella shook her head at ever thinking it was.

Tonight proved he had not the temperament and, even if he did, he was Lord of this manor. He could play the piano all day and all night if he wished. Why would he only play in the darkest night?

He's your brother.

A man never seen, never spoken of, only heard; the mysterious man at the piano who played her to sleep every night.

The man she saw at the cemetery.

A man who was supposed to be dead, visiting his own memorial.

A strange recklessness filled Ella with an anticipation she had never before known. She had to meet him or at least catch a glimpse. Oh, to hear more of his playing, a full sonata without interruption.

Such a talent shouldn't be hidden. He could be the toast of four counties with such ability.

Promises to not ponder things which were of no concern to her, made to her father within the pages of her journal, went by the wayside. A plan started to form in her mind.

Ella left her seat in the school room and picked up the copy of Ivanhoe she had just finished reading. It provided a ready excuse to go to the Earl's library, which she had liberty to do in furtherance of the children's education. And the library adjoined the drawing room, connected by a door she could leave ajar.

If she arrived before the midnight performer, she could listen without him being any the wiser.

She smiled. Today was a very good day indeed.

***

Ella dozed in one of the wing back chairs matching the one Lady Margaret seemed to favor. The fire had burned down to coals but in this cozy little nook before it, the fireplace still radiated warmth. Lulled by the ticking of the drawing room mantle clock, the slow predictable beat of the passing minutes, she almost missed the crisp click of the drawing room door opening, and the soft *tap-tap-tap* of a walking stick progressing unerringly towards her.

Sleep fled. She slowed her breathing to prevent giving away her presence. Ella dared not turn around. Instead, she used her ears to tell her what her eyes could not – the sound of the piano stool pulled out; a soft grunt as a man lowered himself on it; the knock of the stick as it bumped the side of the piano before clattering to the floor; a soft curse at the loss of the stick.

Silence.

Then the opening notes of a sonata, deceptively simple at first and then challenging to even gifted performers. Ella smiled in the dark. She recognized it as a work by Josef Haydn, in C-minor. The fingers that played it were skilled and confident, with sensitivity and deftness of touch. Ella was utterly transported through the *andante con moto* and, by the time the final chord was played, she fought the instinct to burst into applause.

Silence reigned once more and she imagined the player reveling in the unheard appreciation of a phantom audience.

He played a C-minor chord, then C-sharp minor, and Ella held her breath hoping it would be the start of the Beethoven sonata she heard the previous night.

The keyboard stilled.

"You must be the new governess."

Ella's eyes opened wide and, for a fleeting second, she considered not answering – but he knew she was here. She swallowed her fear.

"I am," she answered softly.

"Does the governess have a name?" he enquired lightly and, if she was not mistaken, with a hint of amusement.

"Ella Montgomery."

"Pleased to meet you, Ella Montgomery. My name is Thomas Worsley."

Chapter Nine

Ella found herself momentarily without a voice. She rose from the chair slowly. The room was in complete blackness once she turned away from the fire. She hadn't appreciated how much light the dying coals had cast.

Now, with her back to it, she might have sworn she was completely alone if not for the sound of him breathing and the rustle of fabric as he shifted position on the piano stool. In her mind's eye, she tried to recall the way to the door avoiding the furniture and the musical instruments.

"I... I didn't mean to disturb you. I just wanted to hear you play," she said.

Ella took another tentative step. Her hand brushed against the curved maple of the piano. She took another step forward, working her way around it.

"Don't go."

She halted at his words.

"Stay... please."

His voice, now so much closer as she stood near the instrument, held a note of expectancy.

"I shouldn't."

Ella was conscious of the uncertainty in her voice.

Her eyes had now adjusted to the darkened room. Against the gloom, she could see the vague silhouette of the man at the piano. His curly hair identified him as a Worsley. She recalled the portraits of the two young men in the entrance hall.

He must have taken her long hesitation as acquiescence because he began to play again. Warm resonant notes rose from the soundboard. It was a tune she did not recognize, beautifully melodic and dreamy in its form.

"Thank you…it's been a long time since I had anyone other than Mrs. Mellor to talk to," said Thomas Worsley, and he continued playing.

He did not attempt to engage her in further conversation, and, for her part, Ella remained rooted to the spot, her right hand on the rim of the piano, the left across her stomach.

"You play beautifully," she said after a while, before grimacing to herself for uttering such inanity, but her praise elicited from him a *capriccio*, a skilful showing off before returning to his nocturne.

"Thank you."

"How is it we never hear you play during the day?"

The melody stopped abruptly.

"You *have* met my brother, haven't you?"

Tell me, which of them were you in love with?

Although hours had passed since, the violently spoken words seemed to still echo through the room, then they decayed and the drawing room was silent once more.

"Do you play, Miss Montgomery?"

"I do."

Ella watched him move with great difficulty to the end of the stool.

"Would you care to play a duet?"

The screech of a night owl in the grounds disturbed the silence and it was as though a spell had been broken.

Ella was conscious of being alone in a room with a man who was a stranger to her, but more than that, she was in the presence of the brother of her employer, a gentleman, no less. This was most inappropriate.

She shook her head in mute answer to his question.

"Miss Montgomery?"

It occurred to Ella he couldn't see her in the dark, so she gave voice to her answer.

"No... I... I only wished..."

"... to hear me play," he said, echoing her first words to him.

Thomas rose and Ella prepared to run, but he merely centered himself on the stool once more.

"It was you who opened the room to the drawing room last night, wasn't it?"

"It was me," she confessed.

"Then I shall keep you captive for as long as it takes to play Beethoven again for you tonight, Miss Ella Montgomery, and then you will be free," Thomas said, his voice heavy with self-deprecation. "Return to your seat by the fire."

Ella moved past him, back toward the chair then stopped.

"How did you know I was here?" she asked. "Before, I mean. The room is dark and I was completely hidden in the chair."

He began to play the familiar pianissimo C-sharp octave in the lower register and the higher, hesitant triplet figuration that opened the sonata.

"There is more to what we see than we perceive with just our eyes, Miss Montgomery."

* * *

Ella awoke with a start at the sound of the housemaids entering her room with breakfast and hot washing water.

She suspected only four hours had elapsed between her leaving Thomas Worsley and seeking the sanctuary of her bed. Now the whole prior evening seemed a dream.

She washed and dressed quickly, eating her breakfast in the schoolroom while she set up today's activity. Grace and Louisa would be hosting an at-home for their dolls while learning the etiquette of being good hostesses.

Downstairs, the hall clock struck eight. It was not as late as she thought. Her students would still be at breakfast.

Ella approached the tall multi-paned window. The winter's snow had receded a little further, giving a hint of the spring to come. Out over the dale, the village of Renthorpe was picturesque. Soon she would encourage her girls to sketch and she too would practice with her water colors.

Despite the beautiful view outside, her thoughts remained inward. One little mystery was solved – Thomas Worsley was not dead. He was most certainly alive.

And yet he lived like a recluse in the family home and under sufferance of his brother, the Earl. That revelation only elicited more questions.

Why was Thomas shown as deceased on no less than two public memorials? Was the Earl's jealousy of him such he would banish his own brother? Why did Thomas only play alone in the darkness of night? Blackheath Manor should be filled with music all day long. Why, with the talent Thomas possessed, he could find a patron and perhaps even perform concerts.

Behind Ella, a bright and cheery conversation between Louisa and her sister spilled through into the school room as the girls climbed the stairs with Hester.

"But not all roses are red, you know," said Louisa with authority.

"I know that but you can't be Snow White because you don't have white hair. I can be Rose Red because I have brown hair."

"I have brown hair too. And if you're Rose Red, why can't I be Rose Pink? Because there are pink roses and pink is my favorite color. And you shouldn't be Rose Red, you should be 'Rose Yellow' because that's your favorite color."

As the group entered, Hester struggled to contain her mirth and Ella found herself struggling to suppress a grin too.

"Girls, we'll begin today's lesson by practicing our letters," she told the sisters. "Get started by copying them from the board. I'll be back in a moment."

Ella drew Hester to the far end of the school room.

"What do you know about Thomas Worsley?" she asked in a whisper.

The merry light that always seemed to be in Hester's eyes dimmed.

"Why do you ask?"

"At the church, I saw the memorials honoring Mr. Thomas and Mr. Robert, but I know Thomas is alive!"

Hester's eyes flicked away momentarily as though she was considering what to tell Ella.

It seemed everyone had secrets in Blackheath Manor.

Then the nanny leaned closer.

"Do you swear never to breathe a word of what I'm about to tell you?"

Chapter Ten

"'pon my oath," Ella whispered. "I swear." Hester nodded her satisfaction and looked about before speaking in a low tone.

"This has not been a happy house for many years, even long before the death of the last Earl. Although it is not my place to gossip – particularly about my betters – there are things you should know about this place and about this family if you are going to stay and do right by those girls."

Outside in the passageway, a chambermaid bustled past focused on her duty.

Ella glanced over to Louisa and Grace who remained engrossed in their work, but the distraction of the passing servant had been too much for Hester, and Ella also heard the sound of more approaching footsteps.

The nanny shook her head. "There are too many ears here," she said hurriedly. "Sunday, after church, we'll talk. Meet me on the bench along the river path, past the bakery."

"Nanny Proud."

Mrs. Mellor stood in the school room door.

"You are required downstairs."

* * *

Ella stepped into a shadowed doorway and waited for the footsteps to retreat down the service stairs before softly descending the main stairs. She held a book in her hand once again. Her ruse of going to the library would still serve as her excuse, should she be challenged.

Tonight the moon was full. Light streamed through the partially drawn red velvet curtains and Thomas already there, his back to her. He played idly, again not a tune she recognized. It was haunting, a minor chord underpinning a lighter, almost ethereal melody.

Before she could announce her presence, he spoke.

"I was hoping you would return, Miss Montgomery. I was afraid I had frightened you away."

Ella crossed the threshold from the library to the drawing room, moving closer to the piano.

"It is I who should apologize to you."

"For?"

"Disrupting your practice... For not keeping to my place in the household..."

"And what *is* your place?"

"The place of any governess," she answered with just a little spirit, "neither servant nor family; welcome in the company of neither."

"Then that too is something we have in common."

Thomas pressed forward on the keys harshly. Notes of a new piece reverberated loudly in the room, aggressively phrased chords of a *ballade*, as though Thomas was venting his frustrations. It was loud, recklessly so. If he continued, he would wake the household. Ella was about to tell him so when he stopped, his fingers then worked a softer, sweeter melody. To Ella's mind it seemed the storm of his anger turned to a light shower of rain.

"Now it is my turn to be sorry."

Thomas's apology seemed filled with self-loathing.

Ella was drawn to the pain she heard in his tone and found herself laying a hand gently on his shoulder covered in a worsted wool coat of dark blue.

"Consider the matter forgotten," she told him.

She could not bring herself to look at him. Her eyes followed the arm down to where hands, strong and broad, rested on the keys. His long tapered fingers would span an octave easily.

"You have no sheet music," Ella stated, looking at the empty music rest in front of him.

"I have no use for it."

"Then how do you practice? How do you learn new pieces?"

"Look at me, Miss Montgomery."

His voice, low and rich, was close and Ella found herself breathless. She turned her head and, in the sliver of moonlight, she saw him properly for the first time.

Her first thought was he was the most handsome man she had ever seen. The painting of him in the entrance hall only partly did him justice. Then he turned fully to face her and she saw it – a savage, jagged scar stood out on his cheek and slashed upward into his dark hair.

Did he think that such a mark made him a monster? Did his brother think so?

"Look at me," he insisted.

"I am," she whispered. Her eyes settled on his – a deep brown, the color of oak, another Worsley family trait.

"Do you not see?" he asked, his voice barely above a whisper.

"Your scar?"

"If only that were all..."

"Then what?"

"I am completely blind."

Thomas straightened on the stool. When he spoke again, his voice was stronger, angrier.

"I am the blind and scarred cripple whom my brother detests because of his jealousy. He cannot resent my twin brother, God rest his soul, so he saves a double portion of his hatred for me.

"Do you wonder why I haunt Blackheath as a phantom of night? It is for Louisa and Grace's sake, or so I've been told."

His voice turned bitter, a sneer curled his full lips.

"T'would upset the children to see ugly, scarred, crippled uncle Thomas. He was supposed to be dead along with Robert, but didn't have the good manners to stay in his grave. Now my dear brother and his wife just pretend I am dead and encourage the household, and probably the village itself to do the same."

Thomas turned to the piano and began playing a piece so passionate it further loaded the emotion that filled the drawing room air.

Ella put her shaking hands across her lips, not to still her hands but to stifle a sob. She backed away, felt her leg bump a chair and lowered herself onto it. While the music played, she composed herself so, when the last note decayed, her breathing had returned to normal.

Silence returned, descending like a mist. Thomas remained silhouetted in the light, his chest heaving as he too calmed himself.

"Now you know the darkest secret of Blackheath Manor, Miss Montgomery," he said.

"I have enjoyed our brief time together. But it would be wise to avoid it in the future – for your sake and for the sake of my nieces. They are friendless enough, but knowing you are here to give them the love and nurture they need would place me in your debt."

Her heart squeezed in her chest. She could not leave him like this, a poor soul who suffered needlessly for a lack of compassion. Ella approached him once again and placed a hand on his shoulder. When he didn't move, she knelt to look up at his face.

"And what of you?" she asked.

"I have this," he said and played a *prelude*, a tune so sweet it reminded Ella of a stream tumbling over rocks on a warm summer's day.

"And if William should take away the piano, he cannot take away the music in my head."

Thomas turned his face and looked directly at her with his sightless eyes.

"And he cannot take away the memory our two nights together, Miss Montgomery."

Chapter Eleven

Thomas leaned in further, unerringly finding her lips with his. Passion restrained by convention and circumstances fell like the walls of Jericho. Ella closed her eyes as she put her arms around him, but he was stronger and pulled her close in a full embrace.

His kiss left her breathless and wanting more. When he released her, she gasped for air, panting as though she had just run for her life.

Ella, still panting, opened her eyes.

The golden sun was just peeking over the hills. She sat up, disoriented. It was Sunday morning. The bells of St Joseph's rang out over the dale, calling parishioners to the earliest of the morning services.

The water on the stand was cold enough to wake her fully. It sluiced through her fingers as she splashed it on her face.

Ella caught her reflection in the small mirror of the dresser. She looked as though she had had no sleep at all.

The dream...

It seemed so real. She touched her lips to remind herself it had only been an illusion. Relief warred with disappointment over that fact.

He had told her to not visit him again. If it had been for her sake alone, she might have ignored the warning, but there was Louisa and Grace to consider.

Since the girls' presentation to their father nearly two weeks ago, the Earl had said nothing more to her – indeed she had only seen the man once. Since then, he had been absent, in London on business, according to Hester.

His regiment can damn well look after him. He can go to London and live off the Chelsea Pension.

The overheard words came back as she dressed. Could that be the nature of his 'business' away? The thought of Thomas being taken from his home to live in a barracks troubled her. Ella didn't know much about the Chelsea Pensioners but she doubted he would have access to a piano.

Did Thomas know the plans his brother had for him?

After church, Lady Margaret announced she was going to visit a neighbor and would be taking her daughters with her. Ella swallowed her disappointment. Sunday was her half day off, but even more than that, she had arranged to meet Hester today. Now she would have to accompany Lady Margaret.

"Very good, my Lady," Ella replied, dropping a polite curtsy. "Will Lady Louisa and Lady Grace require anything from the house?"

"No. And you needn't give up your half day. I think it is important the girls spend time with their mother, do you not agree? After all, they grow up too quickly."

There was an edge to the woman's voice. Ella allowed herself to make eye contact and found she was being thoughtfully regarded.

"I concur most wholeheartedly, my Lady. There is no better way for young ladies to learn than from the example of their gracious mother. Lady Louisa and Lady Grace have been practicing their table manners and etiquette; I am confident they will be a credit to you."

Lady's Margaret's face softened somewhat.

"I am glad we are agreed, then."

Ella didn't linger at the house once she had seen Grace and Louisa safely aboard the landau. She was already late for her appointment with Hester.

The apple in her pocket would suffice for her lunch. Taking her sketch pad and charcoals would also do as an excuse should anyone ask about her whereabouts or intentions, and reflected that she was becoming uncomfortably practiced in pre-preparing untruths.

The river that ran through Renthorpe was not a large one but wide enough and slow enough for sailing barges to ply upstream and down, transporting goods. This winter had been mild and the river still flowed.

Ella found the path without difficulty and followed the river downstream to where it wound around a small hill. Up two dozen steep steps, she climbed to where a snow-dusted bench, sheltered in the lea of a stand of trees, overlooked the district.

The bench was empty.

Ella wrapped her coat around herself more securely and took in the view. Drifts of snow still lingered here and there but, seeming untroubled by it all, stood Blackheath Manor. The early afternoon light threw the building in sharp relief. She drew out a charcoal and began sketching. Surely Hester could not be far away.

Soon she had completed the structure of the house from this angle. She identified the gallery on the second floor, the school room on the first and, just hidden by the woodlands that separated the house from the village, were the drawing room and library.

Irresistibly, her mind returned to Thomas. What did he do in his room all day? A pang of sadness ached in her chest. He would never see this view of Blackheath, of the river, of the village. Would his injured leg allow him to even walk this far?

Ella looked at her sketch with a critical eye. It was an adequate representation; her talent in this regard was only fair. With embellishment, it would be a suitable enough to send as a gift to the Bishop and his wife to thank them for their kindness.

The wind changed direction, ruffling the pages of the sketch book. Ella closed it, securing it in her satchel. The sun was well past the high point for the day and was making its downward trajectory to the west, painting the landscape the colors of lilac, mauve and purple.

Hester failed to meet her. Ella tamped down disappointment and hurried before the last of the light disappeared.

Despite most of the Worsley family being away, below stairs was only a fraction less busy than usual. Ella skirted the kitchen in her hunt for Hester. The nanny was not upstairs, nor was she in the servants' hall.

Ella spotted the housekeeper. If anyone would know of Hester's whereabouts it would be her.

"Mrs. Mellor, a word if I may."

The housekeeper raised her chin.

"Some of us are very busy, Miss Montgomery. What do you want?"

"I'm looking for Nanny Proud."

"Nanny Proud is no longer here. She left for her sister's home by coach this morning."

Hot and cold ran through Ella in waves as shock worked its way through her. Why had her only friend here left so abruptly and prematurely?

"I... We... we were supposed to meet today a... and... what about the girls?"

A gleam appeared in Mrs. Mellor's eyes, and suddenly Ella understood.

"You! You made this happen!"

Mrs. Mellor did not attempt to deny it.

"After I spoke to the Mistress, it was decided the house would be better served by Nanny Proud leaving sooner than planned. Why have the expense of keeping her on when the young Misses have a perfectly adequate governess? You *are* adequate, aren't you, Miss Montgomery?"

"But Lady Louisa and Lady Grace loved her, and she loved them. They should have been allowed to say goodbye."

A flash of anger lit the housekeeper's features.

"You're allowed certain liberties as governess, but never forget your place here, Miss Montgomery, and never speak to me like that again or you'll be out with the next coach. Do we understand each other?"

Ella blanched and nodded mutely.

"I'll be keeping my eye on you," Mrs. Mellor added. "Rest assured I will be giving the master a full accounting on his return."

Chapter Twelve

"And where do we find middle-C?" Grace was first to put her finger on the ivory key, pushing it to down to sound the note on the piano.

"Good girl," Ella praised, standing behind the two girls who shared the piano stool. "Now put your thumb there and your fingers on each key."

"Why do the notes only go up to 'G'? There are twenty-six letters in the alphabet," asked Louisa.

Ah, Louisa! Ella mused. The girl would always be a challenge, but her way of looking at the world was a special gift.

"Well?"

"If we used all 26 letters it would make the music very hard to read," replied Ella. "So we have eight whole notes in one octave, which starts and ends with 'C'."

"But why doesn't it start with–"

"An 'A'?" Ella interrupted. She had known the child would ask that. "I'm afraid it just does."

Before Louisa could press for further explanation, Ella leaned between the sisters and played a major scale from middle-C to the next higher C.

"This 'C' here," said Ella, tapping the middle-C and stretching out her pinkie finger to strike the higher note, "and this 'C' here are the same note, but a different pitch, see?"

Louisa and Grace laughed at her pun.

"Now you two can practice your scales. Grace at middle-C, Louise you take the octave lower."

Ella set the metronome to a slow beat to make the practice manageable for their small fingers.

"See how beautiful they sound together?"

The drawing room was different in the daytime with the heavy velvet drapes drawn back to let in light. It seemed much larger now she could take in its high ceilings and its elaborate moldings, the fine oak furniture arranged just so.

But Ella preferred to remember it as it had been when it was dark, intimate and filled with music so passionate that, for one moment in her life, she had truly felt alive.

The time that passed since seemed like a dream. Ella walked through it as if half-asleep and not even the evidence of spring – the drifts of purple crocuses in the nearest garden beds, new leaves emerging on the tall trees bordering the grounds – seemed as vivid as this room had been in the black of that night.

More times than she could count, Ella wished she would 'wake up' in this room with Thomas at the piano playing one of those haunting melodies. She swallowed the emotion rising as a lump in her throat.

"That's enough girls," she said. "Shall I play for you now?"

Two little heads popped up over the piano and nodded eagerly. They climbed down from the stool and settled together on the gold velvet chaise longue.

Ella spread her skirts, sat at the keyboard and ran a gentle hand along the white keys. If she imagined hard enough, she believed she could feel where Thomas had touched them. It was almost like a caress.

One of John Field's nocturnes flowed effortlessly from her fingers, a soft and airy composition most inappropriate for this time of day when usually something livelier would be called for.

She closed her eyes as she played. Ella searched for Thomas in her mind, opening door after door on each floor of the house, willing to see him waiting for her, and the words of *The Song of Solomon* came to her:

> *I opened for my beloved,*
> *But my beloved had turned away and was gone.*
> *My heart leaped up when he spoke.*
> *I sought him, but I could not find him;*
> *I called him, but he gave me no answer.*

"Are you sad, Miss Montgomery?"

Ella started at Grace's voice so close, opening her eyes to find the child standing beside her, brow creased with concern.

"No, my dear, not sad."

"But you're crying. I saw you."

"I cried when Nanny left," added Louisa, joining her sister.

Ella shook her head and continued playing.

"Sometimes there is music which is so beautiful that... it makes you remember..."

"Remember sad things?" asked Grace.

"No, not sad things, just... memories, that's all."

The response, though insufficient, seemed enough for the twins who quickly lost interest in the subject. This afternoon they were to have a riding lesson and were growing more than eager to get outdoors.

She finished playing the piece and decided to release the now thoroughly distracted girls. While Louisa and Grace raced upstairs to change – Ella had long given up telling them to slow down –she tidied the room and gazed at the piano once more.

Oh, Thomas, how can we be under the same roof and be kept so far apart? I've tried, I've tried but you fill my thoughts and dreams. I fall asleep listening to you play. Tell me, do you think of me too?

For a moment, she considered leaving him a note, resting it on the keyboard for him to discover when he opened the fallboard, before letting out a bitter laugh.

Stupid girl – writing a note to leave a blind man.

Dismissing the notion, Ella reached into her pocket and withdrew a handkerchief to dry her tears. Suddenly, she stared at the finely embroidered monogram in the corner – *EJM*, for Ella Jayne Montgomery –and a thought came to her.

She gently rubbed the pad of a finger over it, feeling each letter making itself known to her without sight.

Thomas may not be able to see but he could still *read*. She recalled how he traced the outlines of letters on his churchyard memorial months ago. Did he understand the shapes beneath his fingertips? If so, then surely he would be capable of tracing embroidery and discerning its letters.

She folded the square of linen, keeping the letters to the front and placed it lovingly on the keyboard before shutting the cover. Thomas would find it and know she was thinking of him, she hoped.

Later that night, after she had put the girls to bed and completed planning the lessons for tomorrow, Ella searched her sewing box for a scrap of fabric. Another piece of linen, the remains of an old white petticoat came to hand.

Over dinner, a further idea had risen in her mind.

She would embroider a simple message in white thread and leave it on the keyboard also for Thomas to find.

Semper Fidelis. Always faithful.

The words would let Thomas know she still thought of him, that she was a faithful friend. If he took it, she would know he felt the same. If he didn't, well... she would cross that bridge when she came to it and not before.

Ella set to work by lamplight.

Chapter Thirteen

Dear Ella, Your parcel of 14th inst. was a most welcome arrival. It was kind of you to remember the Bishop and me in your prayers, and your gift of your charcoal sketches of St Joseph's church at Renthorpe and of Blackheath Manor were most gladly received.

We trust you are now well settled into your appointment and the two young charges are thriving under your care.

Please do oblige us with your news by writing often. Your late father is always fondly remembered by us and it is of profound sadness that he was elevated to glory so soon.

Knowing of your love of music, I have taken to enclose a copy of Muzio Clementi's instructional piano pieces that your students may profit from, as well as sheet music for their teacher, just to challenge her.

Should time and circumstances prevail, you must call upon us and play.

God bless and sincere regards,
Prudence Stanton

Ella read the letter over once again, touched by the kindness of the Bishop and his wife. The *Gradus ad Parnassum* would be an invaluable aid.

She leaned across her bed, opened the drawer and withdrew a bundle of letters tied together with a grey ribbon and added this latest to her collection.

Ella kept Clementi's music book with her and flipped through it, identifying works her pupils might attempt. The book also provided the perfect excuse to slip down to the drawing room on the pretext of examining the efficacy of the book for teaching by practicing some of the exercises herself.

Then there was the real reason.

Perhaps an acknowledgement from Thomas awaited her. The morning before last, her handkerchief was not there when she raised the fallboard to begin the girls' music lessons.

For the hundredth time today, Ella reminded herself that just because it had gone didn't mean Thomas had taken it.

An overly zealous housemaid may have opened the piano for cleaning and removed it. If that were the case, the housemaid may decide to keep the linen regardless of whose initials were embroidered on it. Even if Thomas himself found the cloth, it didn't mean he understood the message. And even if he did understand, it did not mean the gesture would be appreciated, let alone reciprocated.

She wondered if she should attempt the second message – Semper Fidelis, 'always faithful' – straight away then thought better of it. No, it would remain securely in her pocket until she knew his feelings on the matter.

So focused on her musings was she, Ella entered the drawing room before realizing that it was occupied.

"Yes?"

Lady Margaret stared at her. So did three other women elegantly dressed in multihued gowns, all of whom sat around a square table. It was then that Ella saw the playing cards and markers.

She had interrupted a dinner party. Ella dropped a hasty curtsy.

"Forgive me, my Lady. I didn't realize you had company," she said, backing towards the threshold. "I... I received a music book from Bishop Stanton's wife and thought I might see if it–"

"Oh, let her play, Margaret," said a handsome middle-aged woman to Lady Margaret's right, speaking over Ella. "It's a dull evening without Edith here. She may be a poor hand at whist, but she does play piano rather well."

"But of course, my dear Georgina, I quite forgot the governess is rather accomplished."

The initial censure in Lady Margaret's eyes faded with the apparent opportunity to add to her reputation as hostess. The woman gave her an indulgent smile. "Of course, that is if you're willing to oblige us, Miss Montgomery."

Ella looked at the piano, and gave another curtsy.

"I hope I can do it justice for you, my Lady."

Conscious of the four sets of eyes upon her, Ella walked to the piano with her head held high and with a slightly shaking hand opened the cover. Lying just above middle-C, across the ebony keys of F-sharp, G-sharp and B-flat, was a white handkerchief.

It wasn't her own.

With a surreptitious motion of her hand, Ella swept the silk fabric into her pocket and opened the lid of the piano stool. One of the first pieces to come to hand was Beethoven's *Seven Bagatelles* – light, easy to play and undemanding to listen to.

In moments, the guests returned to their game and paid Ella no further heed for the rest of the evening, although, for her part, Ella learned Lady Margaret's guests were Lady Georgina, Lady Susannah and Lady Anne.

The long case clock in the hall struck eleven. Over her playing, Ella could hear the sounds of talking outside, muffled and indistinct, but most certainly men's voices.

"That probably means Albert has finished the last of your good brandy, my dear Margaret," said Lady Georgina.

"Which is just as well," chimed in Lady Anne, "because I have been off my game all evening. Profound apologies to you, Susannah. In my defense all I can say is it was just as well we weren't playing for stakes!"

The drawing room door opened. The ladies' conversation quieted and Ella, taking her cue from them, rounded out a passage and stopped playing.

The Earl was red-faced with drink. His aristocratic companions crowding behind him were not much more sober. The smell of cigar smoke on their clothing all but overpowered the scent of perfume in the room.

William Worsley's eyes met Ella's.

"You're out of your place, Miss Montgomery." He turned to his wife and, in the same icy tone, demanded, "What is she doing here?"

Lady Margaret rose from her chair.

"She is keeping us entertained, William. I know you have no taste for music, but it does not mean the rest of us should be deprived of its pleasure."

Tension charged the room. Ella kept her hands folded in front of her and her eyes fixed to the keyboard. How she wished to be invisible at this moment. She listened to chairs scraping back on the carpet and the awkward farewells of guests only too well aware an argument was brewing.

"Miss Montgomery," said Lady Margaret, "you are excused."

Ella turned her face to Lady Margaret. The woman returned a look of... *what?* Resignation was the closest Ella could come to describing the expression.

Before Ella could rise, the Earl erupted in rage.

"Are you deaf as well as stupid? You were told to leave!"

Ella's mind screamed to her body to move, but she was momentarily shocked into motionlessness. Obedience to the command arrived with a rush. Ella raced out of the room without offering a curtsy.

She ran up the stairs to the first floor and rested her head on the schoolroom door breathless, listening to the sounds of a growing argument from the floor below.

She clenched the door knob, feeling responsible but unable to help. Not even her rational mind could talk her out of feeling blame.

Belatedly, she remembered the handkerchief in her pocket. She drew it out as she undressed for the night and left it on the nightstand, refusing to examine it until she had turned out the lamp and pulled the covers up to her chin.

Then she allowed herself to reach and take the cloth.

She kept her eyes closed as she slowly unfolded the silk, feeling its neatly stitched rolled hem around each edge. She traced her finger further in, imagining the world as Thomas must now experience it, through the sense of touch.

Without the aid of sight, she became conscious of the smell of the lamp oil and the burned wick; the faint odor of cigar smoke on her black day dress hung up to air; the feel of the flannel nightdress on her body; the blankets over the top embracing her; the sound of her own breathing and the occasional noise of night creatures calling outside.

Round and round the fabric, her fingers traced until they reached a raised thread. Ella felt the ridges on her fingertips slip slowly over it.

She followed the outline of the thread wherever it went. It seemed strange at first. It made no sense to her so Ella turned the handkerchief and traced it over and over again until the shapes took form in her mind.

TJW.

Thomas James Worsley.

Chapter Fourteen

"I love nights like this. I can play as loud as I wish without being disturbed." As though agreeing with Thomas, lightning from the storm outside flashed and an answering roll of thunder rumbled overhead. He matched it with dramatic crescendo on the keys.

Ella blinked rapidly, disoriented for a moment as another flash of lightning illuminated the drawing room before plunging into darkness once again.

"How do you always know I'm here? Know it's me?"

"I can smell your scent. Lily-of-the-valley. It lingers still on your kerchief. I feel the air move as you walk in the room."

Ella listened to the music he played on the piano. She felt she ought to recognize it, but could not name the composer.

"Will you sit beside me, Miss Montgomery? For all the effort we've gone through to be reunited, it would be pointless for us to sit so far apart."

Ella took his invitation and sat beside him; the heat of his body was warmer than the fire that burned low in the hearth. His shoulder brushed against hers as he continued to play. She breathed in and the undertones of clove and cinnamon filled her nose.

She was here with Thomas by her side, not just in her dreams with his handkerchief under her pillow. There was a tug at her heart that brought emotions to the fore and an awareness to her body she had never before experienced.

Each of her senses but sight and taste were aware of him. Ella felt charged with life as the electricity charged the air.

"Do you know Mozart's *Fugue in G-minor* as a *quatre mains?*"

Ella nodded, then belatedly remembered he could not see her. "Yes," she answered, her voice breathy. She stretched her arms to the keys and found her place.

"Ready?"

Ella struck the first notes with confidence. The first two bars were hers alone before Thomas joined in. Their fingers flirted – moving close, then away, then closer still until they almost touched. She kept her eyes closed. There was no need for sight here. She and Thomas played flawlessly together. It was if they had always done this. When the piece was over, she was breathless.

"More?" he asked and, of course, she accepted.

In deference to her sightedness, he suggested she light a lamp in order to find more *quatre mains* sheet music. They played Bach, Schubert, Czerny, and, at the end of a particularly challenging piece, Thomas laughed. It was a joyous sound, so contagious Ella laughed too. It was a release and, though it was impossible, she felt lighter than air. If not for the arm that he placed around her shoulders, she might just float away like a dandelion seed on the breeze.

The laughter ebbed and his collegial gesture became an embrace as Ella stretched an arm around his back in return. The room was silent but for the sound of the steady pouring rain and the thunder now moving into the distance.

"Do my ugly injuries frighten you, Miss Montgomery?"

The sudden seriousness of the question surprised her. He shifted on the stool slightly to face her and she interpreted his wince as he did so as resulting from putting pressure on his damaged left leg.

Ella studied him in the flickering lamplight. Perhaps it was because he could not see her she was emboldened to raise a hand to his scarred face.

Thomas' breath caught as she touched his forehead just beneath a curl of hair at his scalp and traced the ghostly white scar down to the plane of his cheek, allowing her fingertips to linger there.

"I see nothing ugly about you," she told him. "I see a man who did his duty for his country and has suffered for it."

She ran her hand down his arm and spread her fingers over the top of his hand, hers so much smaller than his.

"I see a man with tremendous talent, a gentle-man..." Emotion made her voice fade away.

"I want to see you," he whispered.

Tears sprang to her eyes.

"How?"

Thomas leaned in closer. Ella felt his breath on her cheek and gooseflesh grow across her arms.

"Let me touch you... Ella..."

Her Christian name on his lips brought heat to her cheeks. Her hands shook although she scarcely knew why, so she folded them in her lap. With the assistance of his stick, Thomas stood then let go of the cane, leaning a thigh against the side of the piano for support. He gestured to take both her hands in his and urged her to stand.

One hand approached her cheek and hesitated. He was waiting for her, his uncertainty endearing him to her more with each moment.

"Yes."

Although he didn't need to, Thomas closed his eyes and raised his head. His fingertips found her cheek and his hand cupped it momentarily. Gentle fingertips traced the line of her jaw and down the column of her neck. Ella closed her own eyes and swallowed her nerves.

"Nervous?" he asked. A second hand joined the first, caressing both cheeks at once before they moved to the back of her head and settled on the nape of her neck with a touch so light a sigh seemed the only appropriate response.

"I'll let you in on a secret," he continued. "I'm nervous too."

Ella found herself unable to speak, overwhelmed by the sheer intimacy of the act. No one had ever touched her like this. She felt her cheeks bloom with heat.

Thomas's hands returned to her face, his thumbs stroking her forehead before they followed the shape of her nose and tugged along her lips which opened of their own accord.

"Beautiful," he exhaled. "You're even more beautiful than I imagined when I only had your voice in my head."

Ella's cheeks heated further. Only her father had called her beautiful, although she never believed it. She was always the plain one, the one whom potential suitors would overlook for more comely girls.

The tremors that had started in her hands now affected her body. She breathed in deep to mute the gasp heralding an impending avalanche of emotion. Her efforts were in vain.

"Oh, darling Ella."

Thomas enfolded her into his arms.

She felt the soft white linen of his shirt at her cheek and opened her eyes. The scent of him up close, all warm spice, was even more intoxicating. She hugged him tightly, as though through such an act they could merge into one – one body, one soul, one mind, that she could be one with him.

Emboldened by her reaction, Thomas's hands explored the length of her back from her shoulder blades to her hips, and then along the line of her waist, stopping before they reached the underside of her breasts.

Thomas was breathing hard. He drew back slightly and shook his head as though to clear it.

"There's so much I want..." he paused. "... I have to stop before I compromise you further than I've already done."

He straightened and took a halting step back.

"I can't tell you how much joy you've brought to my existence in such a short space of time. I'm in a house filled with people but I'm so lonely. Those who attend me do so out of duty. I might as well be the ghost my brother wishes. Thank you for seeing *me*... I don't know how I can repay you."

Love, desire, compassion, want... none of the words in her lexicon were adequate to describe Ella's feelings at that moment. She craved him in the same way she craved air, needed him in a way that was new and strange to her.

"There's one way," she said, breaching the gap and taking his hands as he had taken hers.

"Will you kiss me, Thomas?"

Chapter Fifteen

"If I kiss you, I won't be able to stop." Thomas made his warning clear. Ella ignored his words, raising her hands until they met behind his head and urged him to her.

Her experience with kisses was non-existent. Kissing the cheek of her father or her elderly aunt was hardly preparation for this moment.

Although she didn't know the exact way of it precisely, Ella found herself driven by an instinct she didn't know she possessed.

His lips, when they met hers, were soft and tentative at first but, as hers parted ever so slightly, Thomas seemed to acquire a confidence and, with gentle pressure, coaxed them a little further apart.

The feel of his tongue on her lips was shocking at first but it sent a sensation through her that settled low in her belly – an anticipation for something outside of her experience but it was something she knew she wanted to experience with Thomas.

Their kisses became more powerful, more demanding, desire stretching her nerves taut. She pressed herself against him and felt something below his waist stir. She ought to be shocked by it but she wasn't. Behind her own closed lids, she saw fireworks and somehow understood this was a prelude to something more.

"Please Ella, have mercy on a man's soul."

Thomas took a step back and found the edge of the piano to steady himself. His other hand pulled hers from his neck. He brought it to his lips, lavishing ever more passionate kisses on it.

Ella blinked rapidly as though returning to herself. Now she could hear again the falling rain outside and the harsh breathing of the man before her. Her world, which seemed full of vibrant color in the moments before, returned to just a darkened drawing room.

A lump of ice now formed in her throat.

"You must think me the most..." Ella found herself lost for words once again. *Forward* was the least her conscience accused her of; a woman of easy virtue, a strumpet, a wanton – all of those she believed were more adequate descriptions of her behavior.

Thomas shushed her with a gently raised finger of admonishment.

"Tell me the color of your hair."

The unexpected question caught her off-guard. Ella lowered herself to the piano stool. Its creak under her weight indicated the way and Thomas joined her.

"My hair?" she replied at last. "It's... it's brown."

"Brown? As the color of oak or like the color of an old penny? Or perhaps brown like the color of almonds?"

"I don't know... it's just medium brown I suppose."

"Describe it for me. Find a parallel."

Ella closed her eyes, embarrassed at being unable to describe such a simple thing she saw every day in the mirror. At least Thomas couldn't see the depth of her shame at her behavior.

She thought on her answer and wrinkled her nose at the only description that would come to her.

"It's the color of well brewed tea. With milk. But not too much, just a drop."

She expected him to laugh; instead he looked thoughtful.

"And your eyes?"

"Hazel."

He reached out a hand to stroke her cheek once again before struggling to his feet. He felt for his walking stick leaning against the side arm of the keyboard and moved out from behind the stool. She rose and watched him walk unerringly to the drawing room door where he turned back to her.

"If I were a true gentleman, I'd walk you home to your door but it's safer if you go there alone by the main staircase," he said. "I use the servants' stairs – they're right next to my room on the same floor as yours. The staff are long used by my nocturnal habits. No one ever pays me any mind."

Ella crossed the room to him and raised a hand to his shoulder. She squeezed it in a silent good night before stepping around him to reach for the door. Thomas stayed her hand with such a confident reach that, for a moment, Ella imagined he saw her.

"Before we go on," he cautioned her, "I need to know you're aware of the consequences if we are discovered. I have nothing to offer you, not a single thing my brother could not take away from me – except you. If we're found out, you will lose your position, your reputation and the roof over your head, and you would be vulnerable to every predator lurking among the male of our species."

Thomas shook his head sorrowfully.

"I should have remained firm in my resolve to stay away from you but such thought makes my bleak life even more miserable. Can you forgive me?"

Ella fell into his arms, an embrace of comfort rather than passion, a union of two lonely souls who in the moment had found a light in the darkness.

"If you are weak, then I am also. My waking moments are consumed with waiting for our time together. Please don't send me away. Dearest Thomas, it would be more than I could bear. Living at Blackheath would be impossible."

"Darling Ella," he sighed, placing open-mouthed kisses in her hair. After a moment, he ended their embrace, his hands lingering on her shoulders.

"I'll remain here and wait a while, then play you a lullaby to send you sweet dreams."

Thomas smiled, and kissed her chastely on the cheek before whispering good night.

He opened the door and stood aside for her to leave but she paused.

"Why did you want to know the color of my hair and my eyes?"

"So I can imagine them as I make love to you in my dreams."

Chapter Sixteen

Ella only pretended to study the view back across the river to Blackheath. Spring was in full flower and today was an especially beautiful mid-May day but she didn't see the blue sky, the riot of nodding yellow daffodils, or the line of little cygnets on the river swimming dutifully behind two elegant white swans.

From her vantage point on the hillside bench, her entire focus was on two figures in black walking arm-in-arm on the well-beaten riverside path just five hundred yards away below. It was Thomas and Mrs. Mellor.

It appeared they had taken the long way around rather than the short cut through the woods, and would soon leave the path to make their way up to St Joseph's church cemetery.

Of the pair, Thomas was her only focus. He walked with his cane, his gait uneven. She might have been able to make out his features even at this distance but his face was once more obscured by a hat pulled low over his eyes. One part of her mind was consumed with jealousy. It should be her walking alongside him, describing the scenery, listening to him as he identified a bird by only two notes of its call. The other, more reasoning part reminded her Thomas was grateful for the housekeeper's kindness. If not for her, he would not leave the house at all.

The better angel of her nature won, but it was a hard fought battle that gave her little comfort. Did he somehow know she was near? If she called out might he hear? So might Mrs. Mellor.

She hastily sketched the scene below with her charcoal but rather than at a distance it was in a closer view. The man on her sketchpad was whole and his cane was used for debonair effect. The woman at his side was her, in a summer dress, the neck scooped low to show a cameo at her throat.

"Miss Montgomery, you're in love!" proclaimed Grace beside her suddenly.

Ella knew her own startled reaction expressed itself on her face as she turned to the child because the youngster frowned and pulled back the tiny buttercup flower in her hand.

"That's wrong," Louisa said, confidently correcting her sister. "Yellow under the chin means she likes butter, not that she likes boys."

Grace made a small moue of disdain as she rejoined Louisa in the task of gathering wildflowers for today's art lesson.

"Miss Montgomery can like boys too if she wants," Grace retorted.

Louisa was of a mind to disagree. "She's a *governess*. She's not supposed to like boys."

Ella's heart started beating in her chest once more.

"She is the cat's mother," she told Louisa. "Young ladies use proper names to describe people." It was not the first time she had corrected the girls on the topic of manners in speech and, to an extent, her correction was reflexive.

However, it also seemed a good way to encourage them to change the subject, and Ella was relieved when Louisa evidently thought it wise to do so.

She approached and peered over Ella's shoulder to look at her sketch.

"That was Mrs. Mellor on the path but your picture doesn't look like her. You've made her young and pretty."

Out of the frying pan and into the fire...

Ella thought quickly.

"Art is as much about imagination as it is about capturing what is really there."

"Oh..." said Grace. "Does that mean my cornflower can be red if I want it to be?"

Ella assured her it *could* be red if she wanted to make it so, but it would no longer be a cornflower. Then a question came unbidden to her lips and was spoken before she evaluated the wisdom of it.

"Do you know the man who walks with Mrs. Mellor?"

Ella observed the twins looking to one another, then back to her, their eyes falling. After a momentary silence, broken by the call of the swans, Louisa spoke up.

"He's the ghost who lives in our house."

The words were spoken so gravely by the child that the resulting laugh threatening to bubble out of Ella's mouth somehow seemed wholly inappropriate, so she swallowed it.

"Who told you he was a ghost?" she asked instead.

"Papa did," said Grace.

Ella was shocked and tried not to let the emotion show in her voice. "Why did he do that?"

"Well, we hear him at night and ghosts come out at night. And once Louisa and I wanted to see, so we got out of our beds and we saw him on the landing. Father saw him too and told us he was a dead man."

"And ghosts are dead men," chimed Louisa, completing the circle of their logic.

"I don't understand why your brother would say such a hateful thing," said Ella softly, keeping her voice down.

She lay on the chaise longue, her eyes closed, with the soothing nocturne Thomas played washing over her.

"It's an apt description considering I haunt the manor at night," he replied, transitioning with an arpeggio to a new piece in a different key.

"Other families who lost sons and brothers in the wars with Napoleon would rejoice to have one return home," said Ella, "*not* pretend to the world he's dead."

"The Worsleys are not like other families. Besides, William has many good reasons to wish me dead."

"You jest."

Thomas's fingers stilled on the keyboard.

"Not quite. You know all the secrets of Blackheath Manor but one. I've scarce thought about it in four years myself." He paused briefly before continuing. "William is my younger brother."

Ella sat up with a gasp.

"But that means…"

"Yes. By rights, I should be the Earl of Renthorpe."

Chapter Seventeen

Ella's pulse pounded in her ears, the rushing blood making her nearly deaf to Thomas's next words as she found him sitting beside her, holding both hands in his.

"Months ago, I said you knew the secrets of Blackheath Manor." He waited for her to acknowledge him. Ella squeezed his hands by way of response, then let them go.

"It was the truth, but it was not the whole of it."

With one arm around her shoulder, he urged her back to rest against his chest. She scarce knew what to say. Thomas brought up his hand to stroke her hair. He remained silent for long moments and she could imagine him carefully composing words in his head.

"I had wondered whether you truly understood the significance of the family portraits in the entrance hall," he started. "There was an elder brother, George – our father's heir. Robert and I were young hellions, utterly inseparable as I imagine Louisa and Grace to be... William was the youngest of us all.

"Younger sons have few prospects, but Robert and I had a taste for adventure. We joined a small number of our peers as officers and, in the spring of 1815, we joined the 69th Brigade.

"A few months later, we were at the battle of Quatre Bras. It was very nearly a complete rout. The head of the

Dutch forces was William, the Prince of Orange. He countermanded an order from our General to form a defensive square and prepare for attack.

"Robert and I were side by side in a single formation when Napoleon's cavalry cut through us like butter. Our commander was killed.

"The last thing I remember seeing with certainty was Robert looking at me in surprise and the bloom of red across his chest as he fell. Then I was struck also. I've never known such pain. I thought my head had been cleaved in two. As it turned out, it wasn't far from the truth."

Thomas paused in his recounting.

"I believe I was unconscious for a time. At least until nightfall. I have the vaguest memory of seeing tall thin trees above me and restless stars across a darkening sky as they carried me from the field. Then nothing for a very long time and, when I was aware again, I could see no more."

Ella closed her eyes and could see the battle as vividly as though she had been there herself. She nuzzled his chest, listening to the beat of his heart. She thanked God with each one he had survived.

"This is no topic for a lady, I'm sorry–"

"No," Ella interrupted, her voice hoarse from restrained emotion. "I want to hear it. I want to know everything about you."

She felt his lips in her hair. One arm slid across her waist, holding her to him, while the other traced gentle strokes across her cheek.

"Two days later, as Wellington was winning the Battle of Waterloo, our father and George were killed when a bricks kiln they were inspecting exploded.

"Blackheath was already in mourning when William received mistaken word that Robert and I had been killed also.

"He believed he had gone from being fourth child to Earl within a mere three days. It wasn't his fault; he just didn't know I was really still alive."

"Surely you're not apologizing for him," Ella observed, unable to keep the sharp note from her voice.

Thomas sighed deeply.

"Perhaps I am. I suspect in some ways he never wanted to be Earl. Certainly, he was never brought up for it, nor for the responsibilities it entailed.

"Six months later, word arrived I was alive but gravely ill, and not expected to live. It must have been easier for William to keep pretending I was dead and, by the time I was returned home, I had pneumonia and wished I *had* died.

"I had difficulty speaking... I distinctly remember between fever dreams hearing the doctor tell William the head injury had turned me into an imbecile on whom treatment ought not be wasted."

Tears rolled down Ella's cheeks and she let them fall silently.

"At that time, I was as helpless as an infant. My left leg had been crushed on the battlefield. I couldn't see. I could barely make my mouth form intelligible words. It was Mrs. Mellor who took pity on me. For six months,

I lay in my bed in a world of my own and, for want of anything else, I dreamed of music. I wrote cantatas, sonatas, nocturnes, even entire symphonies in my head.

"My music master used to call me an idler, and I was, but I never forgot the lessons and the discipline he instilled. I bargained with God each night to give me one more dawn to complete my works, then the strength to sit at a piano and then the dexterity in my fingers to play it again.

"One more day became one more week, became one more month, then one more year."

Warmth grew in Ella's chest. Night after night she had wondered about the dreamy, romantic music he played so confidently – rich with harmonies and soaring melodies, but unknown to her.

They were his own work.

Thomas sat up and groped on the floor for his stick. After a moment's struggle, he rose to his feet and went back to the piano where he started playing a lullaby. Ella joined him at the stool.

"What are you going to do with your compositions?"

"Other than play them?"

Ella heard the tease in his voice.

"Yes! They're beautiful and other people should hear them."

"Under present circumstances, such an outcome is unlikely."

"But not impossible."

Thomas brought his hands down on the keys jarringly, with an ill-concealed anger.

"I'm an ugly, blind cripple who the world thinks is dead, Ella."

"But..."

"No!"

Ella started at the vehemence. Thomas was immediately apologetic.

"I'm sorry," he whispered. "I shouldn't have shouted."

He turned his head toward her. Ella could feel his breath on her cheek, but she could not look at him, not without turning to tears once again. She could not. Would not.

When she did not respond, Thomas sighed and returned to a familiar etude.

"However imperfect the situation, that is the reality of my life here at Blackheath," he continued.

"If I am a prisoner here, I am a willing one. If I am a living ghost, perhaps it's better I remain so.

"For the sake of Margaret and the children I wouldn't risk a scandal by revealing my existence to the wider world. It would blight their lives and for what? A title I have no use for and responsibilities I can't fulfill?

"Despite William's empty threats every so often to throw me on the mercy of the Chelsea Pension, you must believe me; I have been content – until now."

Thomas's voice dropped an octave to deliver the last two words. Ella turned at them and found herself mesmerized by his dark rich eyes, the sensuous fullness of his mouth. She unconsciously licked her lips. They tingled in memory of the previous kisses.

As though Thomas already knew, he leaned closer still and she met his lips. Ella sighed into his open mouth as he started his ravishment of hers. He tasted her lips and her tongue, kissing her so thoroughly she only remembered to breathe when her lungs burned for lack of air.

Leaving her mouth, his lips blazed a trail across her cheeks and to the sensitive column of her neck where sensation flew across every nerve. Thomas's tongue lavished attention on her ear lobe. His breathing, as harsh as hers, swirled in the shell of her ear.

"You shouldn't have offered me hope for anything more than my life as it was, Ella," he whispered. "It makes me think very dangerous thoughts."

Chapter Eighteen

Blackheath Manor, sitting in a low hanging early morning mist, receded in the distance. The cart beneath Ella swayed its way down the lane leading the party from the house to nearby Dunstable for the day. It was the third Wednesday of the month and her full day of liberty.

Normally Ella looked forward to it.

She would sit at a tea house and indulge in a pastry and write her letters, then idly browse the shops looking at pretty gowns she could not afford on her thirty pounds a year.

In the end, she would settle for a few ribbons, some little trinkets for the girls, and, once, some fabric with which she had intended to fashion a new gown – a task that would nearly be completed if not for a certain distraction.

Now, leaving the red brick mansion seemed like she was leaving a part of herself behind.

After she parted from Thomas last night, she had wrestled with his words.

If I am a prisoner here, I am a willing one.

Why would someone choose not to pursue liberty? Thomas could be free. He could order anyone of the servants to take him anywhere he wished to go, and yet...

As the last of the view of Blackheath disappeared around a sweep in the road, she understood.

Ella would rather be there with him instead of at liberty on this beautiful spring day. She too would be a willing prisoner if it meant they would be together.

She listened idly as two housemaids also on their day off gossiped with a couple of kitchen maids who were accompanying the cook to the markets. A groomsman joined them in the back. He tried to catch the eye of an upper housemaid who was doing her best to both express her interest and ignore him at the same time. The cook sat beside the driver, who was a man of about the cook's age. Sitting side by side, they looked like the old married couple they were.

Ella might have been content to remain alone with her thoughts, ignored by the others as she so frequently was, but a question burned within her.

How many of them knew Blackheath's secret? Did they care? Was it a threat of dismissal alone which held their tongues?

"What happened to the Earl's twin brothers?"

The question was out of her mouth before the words had formed in her mind. Conversation died and five pair of eyes stared back at her.

"They died in the war, Miss," answered the upper housemaid at last. "There be a memorial to them in the churchyard. Surely you ain't been here for near on six months and not seen it?"

The young woman's pale blue eyes seemed to ask a question of their own. Ella looked at the others by turn and silent reproach met her. Her fate as an outsider had been sealed.

The awkward silence in the end was broken by the driver who started whistling a tune, then one by one the passengers started singing.

Good morning, pretty maid,
Where are you going?
To range these fields so fair,
There's no man knowing,
I think too bold you are,
To range these fields so fair,
In danger everywhere,
Thou charming maiden.

A charming maid I am,
Sir, she replied.
Without any guile or care,
To no man tied;
My recreations are, to range
These fields so fair;
To take the pleasant air,
Thou boasting stranger.

Ella slid thruppence across the counter along with her monthly letter to Mrs. Prudence Stanton and waited for the clerk behind the counter to check whether there was any mail that waited for her. The bespectacled young man, with pale blond hair so thin it almost seemed he was bald, returned with two envelopes.

"Two this month, Miss Montgomery," he said, glancing at them. "I hope it's not another admirer. Against one I might stand a chance, but two..."

This clumsy and decidedly one-sided flirtation had been going on for months and the clerk had yet to tire of it. Ella merely smiled and shook her head. She left and crossed the road over to the tea rooms.

She recognized the writing on the first letter immediately. It was from the Bishop's wife. The writing on the second envelope was not at all familiar. Ella opened it first. Out slipped a note.

Dear Miss Montgomery,

I thought long about writing you this letter.

You see, I felt very ill-used at my sudden dismissal from Blackheath Manor. On the journey to my sister's in Harrogate, I determined I would reveal every last secret of the Worsley family. I spent my first week writing it all down.

But spring did warm more than just ground. It warmed my heart too and since I was so well settled in my new life, I had second thoughts about writing to you. But then I thought of those beautiful girls – little Gracie and little Louisa (if you would write me news of them, I'd be grateful), and of another poor soul, the existence of whom you seemed to be aware.

I remembered that I told you if you were to do right by those girls then you would need to know the full story and so it is enclosed, best to my recollection.

I ask just one more thing in return – let no one see this but yourself.

With greatest sincerity,
Hester Proud (the nanny).

The subsequent missive was four densely written pages, scribed both sides with the occasional ink blot making some words indecipherable. Even without the covering letter, it was evident in the tight, sharp strokes of the pen that the writer was one in a great temper at the time.

Much of it contained news she already knew – the death of the old Earl and his heir, the existence of Thomas and the devotion of Mrs. Mellor to his care; even the antipathy of the young Earl towards his own family was not news to her, but in the middle of the third page came this revelation:

I have been a part of a great deception, God forgive me, but it was done with the very best of intentions.

This I have not breathed to another living soul. The March of 1815 was the last month at Blackheath where all of the Worsley men were under the same roof. Robert and Thomas were off to war soon, and the old Earl and George were dead before summer came.

Lady Margaret Carlton (as she was then) was just seventeen. She had a fondness for Robert, although she pretended she couldn't tell the difference atwixt him and Thomas, being as they were twins. And they was off to serve Wellington.

I knew Margaret was with child even before she realized. I also knew the youngest Worsley brother was besotted with her.

Who knew when Robert would be back, if at all? God rest him. I was the one who persuaded Lady Margaret to set her cap at William and marry him with all haste for the sake of the child she carried and her reputation. She grew larger than expected for the length of time we calculated she had been pregnant. We two conspirators did our best to keep this secret.

And we were successful too, but I wonder at what cost?

Chapter Nineteen

L ong shafts of golden afternoon light flickered through the trees as the day party from Blackheath made their way home again.

Ella was squeezed between a large sack of potatoes and two large barrels of salted fish, out of direct view of anyone else. They were too engrossed in their own chatter anyway to pay her any attention.

Oh, Thomas...

Did he know or at least suspect the paternity of his nieces?

She instinctively knew he did and sensed it was another link in the chain irrevocably binding him to the walls of Blackheath.

Ella closed her eyes and rested herself against the sack. One of Thomas' cantatas came to mind; the shadowy form of his hands as he performed in the semi-darkness of the drawing room she mimicked on her lap as the cart lurched towards Renthorpe.

Prudence Stanton would enjoy this piece, she thought absently. It was to her taste.

It seemed so unfair! Thomas was too good a musician, too good a composer to go unrecognized even if only by the society around the district.

The sun sank over the hills, leaching the sky of color and giving it all to the clouds in regal reds, golds and purple. Ella did not see it. Instead, she saw crotchets, quavers, semibreves – each note dropping on staff paper like a rain on dry earth, bringing it to life.

And with the falling notes formed a plan.

Thomas might never be free from Blackheath, but his music could be.

It was Saturday afternoon and, since William would be spending yet another overnight in London, Lady Margaret had accepted a weekend invitation to her sister's home and would take her daughters with her. Ella was informed by Mrs. Mellor her services would not be required for the visit.

Blackheath Manor seemed somehow brighter without the family in residence. After the noon meal, the house was virtually silent. It seemed more like a half holiday.

Ella frowned, concentrating over the piano. She played a few bars before stopping and marking them in pencil, recalling the progression of Thomas's cantata from memory.

It was slow progress and much harder than she thought it was going to be. Ella returned to the keys and played another three bars. She had been working on this particular passage for the better part of an hour and it still didn't sound correct. Ella tried the chord again.

"Try B-natural."

Ella jumped, knocking the stool over and tipping the lid of the piano shut with a bang. Thomas winced at the sound.

"What are you doing?" Thomas asked, his voice deceptively mild. He stepped forward and closed the drawing room door.

"I could ask you the same thing," Ella muttered, righting the stool and collecting the spilled sheet music. "You're never down here during the day. What if someone sees you?"

"Mrs. Mellor told me I would have the house to myself. And you never answered my question. What are you doing?"

Ella was struck mute. In the bright afternoon light, she saw him clearly for the very first time. The broad white scar on his face was more pronounced than could be seen by lamplight. It slashed down below his cheek and disappeared beneath the collar of his linen shirt which was loosely laced at the neck. Thomas's stick tapped lightly on the furniture as he made his way towards her.

"Ella?"

"I'm here," she told him and laid a hand on his forearm.

"I was afraid the beauty had fainted dead away in the presence of the beast."

Ella stepped closer.

"Then you must not remember the tale well. The beauty may have been startled, but she was never afraid of the beast."

Thomas pulled her into his arms and they held each other for a long, silent moment. Such a simple action and Ella felt a stirring within her body. Embraces in the dark were one thing but in the daylight with the outside world in view, it seemed a much more daring act.

"I was trying to transcribe your cantata. My father's superior, the Bishop, and his wife love music. I thought they would like yours."

Deep creases formed between Thomas's eyebrows.

"And who were you going to say was the author of the piece?"

"You, of course."

Thomas shook his head gravely.

"No."

Ella looked down at the piece of paper she held in her hand. Of course, she couldn't. What was she thinking? Thomas Worsley was dead; to resurrect him would be to ruin lives and cause a scandal that would reverberate long into the future, affecting the prospects of Grace and Louisa.

"I... That was very presumptuous of me. I'm sorry."

"Yes, it was, but don't be sorry," he smiled. "Searle. Thomas Searle."

"I beg your pardon?"

"Searle was my mother's maiden name. Use that," he said, edging past her to the piano. Thomas made a couple of unsuccessful swings of his hand to find the misplaced stool before he grabbed it and dragged it to the correct position.

"I've been thinking a lot about what you said. I would be lying if I said I didn't want people to hear my music. I don't want my only mark on the world to be a lie chiseled in granite in a graveyard. Will you help me publish my music?"

Ella smiled with delight. She threw her arms around Thomas and kissed him numerous times on his cheek and temple.

"Yes! Absolutely yes!"

"Again?"

Ella sat alone at the piano and played the cantata from beginning to end for the second time. When the last of the notes faded, she turned on the stool to look at Thomas where he reclined on the gold velvet chaise longue and waited for his judgment. It came in the form of a beaming smile.

"That's it! You've done it!"

Ella looked at the sheets of freshly transcribed music. They had begun with a short but atmospheric nocturne before taking on the complexity of the cantata with its greater length.

"A nocturne and the cantata. Do you think it's enough?" she asked.

"It's enough for today. Whether they are *good* enough will be for others to decide."

"Nervous?"

Thomas looked as though he was about to speak then paused. He stood up and walked to her as fast as his injured leg would allow. Ella stood also.

"I can hear the servants coming back. I should go."

Thomas kissed her on the lips then clasped her hands in his, kissing one, then the other.

"Meet me here tonight?"

Ella gave her promise and watched him leave the drawing room, listening to the soft tap of his stick as he walked through the hall and up the main stairs, avoiding the servants' stairs for once.

Now her ears had become attuned to what Thomas had heard – the sudden burst of faint laughter, a distant clash of pots from the scullery, the slam of a door closing in the wind. Altogether, they were the ordinary sounds of servants careless in the absence of their masters– and yet there was something odd.

Ella shrugged off the feeling.

She gathered their afternoon's work and was about to leave the room when it struck her -- Thomas had closed the door behind him when he came in, but when he left, the door was ajar as he approached it.

Had someone been listening in? Was someone spying on them?

Surely not. She would have seen. Thomas would have *heard*.

Another door slammed shut from elsewhere in the house.

It was nothing, Ella assured herself.

It was just the wind.

Chapter Twenty

It was a simple tune in the key of C. Ella played the melody through once with her right hand while tapping a finger of her left hand to perform a count in. She nodded to Louisa who was a study in concentration.

"Frère Jacques, frère Jacques, dormez vous? Dormez vous..."

She gave the girl an encouraging smile and pointed to Grace who sang her opening lines. Ella joined in last. They sang the round through twice before Grace stopped with the giggles.

"We did it! We did it right this time, Miss Montgomery!"

The little girls' enthusiasm was infectious and Ella joined in their applause.

"Well done, you both did very well," she said. "But to make sure we perform it well on the night we will need to practice every day from now until the party."

The Worsley's summer party in August was the biggest social event held at Blackheath Manor each year. Last week when Louisa and Grace were demonstrating what they had learned for the Earl and Countess, William proclaimed he expected his daughters ready to perform for their guests.

The thought they would be allowed to stay up to see the beautiful ladies in gowns and jewels thrilled the girls and it took them many hours afterward before Ella could persuade them to sleep.

Now the soiree was just four weeks away.

At the sound of rattling cutlery, Ella looked up and acknowledged the housemaid who brought a tray into the drawing room and set it on a side table.

"After we've had our morning tea," said Ella to the children, "we shall practice our piano pieces but, since it is a very lovely day, shall we take our tea on the terrace?"

The suggestion was accepted enthusiastically. The girls skipped through the French doors. Ella picked up the tray to follow when she heard a voice behind her.

"A moment, Miss Montgomery."

Ella turned and gave Lady Margaret a curtsy made awkward by the tray in her hands.

The Countess looked younger in her morning dress of pretty multi-colored flowers of green, pink and purple. Ella reminded herself she and Lady Margaret were about the same age.

She stood and waited for her to speak. She seemed to hesitate as though gathering her thoughts.

"I just want to be sure the girls are happy, Miss Montgomery," said Lady Margaret at last. "My husband is... an *exacting* man, and I fear he does not understand little girls. I want to be certain he is not demanding more than their age and abilities allow."

"Your daughters are intelligent children, my lady," Ella answered honestly. "It is my honor to help bring out their gifts."

There was a yearning in the woman, Ella could sense it. It floated just below the surface of her beautifully composed countenance. Lady Margaret wished to be a mother to her children. Ella found an inkling of kinship with the woman before her.

A thought occurred to Ella and it seemed right.

"Would you like to have morning tea with us?" she suggested politely. "I know Lady Louisa and Lady Grace would be delighted to have their mother join them."

The delight on Lady Margaret's face brought sunshine into the room as she accepted the invitation. Ella rang for a maid to bring another setting and followed Lady Margaret onto the terrace.

She watched her with her daughters and saw the woman who seemed listless and unanimated in her habitual seat beside the fire each evening enlivened now in the company of her children. Ella suddenly appreciated what a beautiful young woman Lady Margaret was.

No wonder the young William Worsley was besotted with her before the woes of family deaths and the obligations of his unwanted elevation embittered him. And his brother Robert too – he had loved her also, Ella considered – then came a further thought.

Had Thomas? Was that another reason he stayed?

"I understand there's a wedding portrait in the hall. Has Margaret changed much since that?" asked Thomas. He sat at the piano playing the left hand portion of one of his nocturnes, a piece which was a mixture of melancholy and hope.

Ella was seated at a small table set beside the piano stool, transcribing the notes. She lay the pen down and considered his question which had been prompted by her mention of the morning tea.

"She is still a beautiful woman but if I were to compare her with the portrait in the hall, I would say she looks less happy. It shows around her eyes."

Thomas acknowledged the answer with a nasal *hmmm* and continued playing the right hand. The question Ella had wanted to ask all night would no longer be silent.

"Did you love her?"

"I think we were all in love with Margaret then," he answered plainly, and swept into the full piece from its beginning. The left hand arpeggios allowed his right hand to explore the higher keys freely, soaring into beautiful melodies that touched her heart as her eyes followed the sheet music.

"But that wasn't the question you really wanted to ask me," he said at last.

Ella's cheeks flushed and for once she was glad he could not see her.

He was right. There was just one question Ella wanted the answer to, but she could never pose it. She had no right to the answer despite her own feelings. Her body and soul were attuned to him and longed for him when daylight parted them. She was in love with Thomas, utterly and completely.

Her emotions were too raw, far too close to the surface for her to remain so near to him. She rose and set the table aside, gathering up their night's work. This was the ninth composition transcribed. Tomorrow, Ella would go to Dunstable and post the package of works to the publisher in London.

"I should go," she whispered, turning towards the door.

"Ella?"

Thomas had risen and was right behind her. His hand grasped her upper arm.

Ella refused to turn toward him and she remained facing the door. She closed her eyes at the touch of his fingers caressing her cheek. Tender fingertips traced along the clenched muscle of her jaw, the line around her mouth which held her mouth closed against the sob burning behind it.

"Don't leave me... please."

His words whispered close to her ear brought her undone. The leaves of sheet music slipped from her hands to the floor.

"Oh, Thomas, my love."

Her words were barely audible, but Thomas heard them and pulled her back against him. He leaned down and placed hot kisses on the sensitive nape of her neck, sending shivers of desire all the way down to her bare toes which curled in the thick rug on the floor.

"Until you arrived I was in a miserable half existence," he said, his voice hoarse. "You brought me back to life, Ella. I want to feel the sun on my face with you in my arms. I want to see the world through your eyes... I want to spend the rest of my life with you.

"I love you."

His declaration opened a well-spring and Ella's held-back sob became a long sigh. Thomas's right arm slid around her waist. His long fingers splayed across her stomach then moved higher, touching the underside of her breasts.

Desire filled every part of her as he kissed and caressed her with the same passionate abandon with which he played his music.

Then he stilled. The scent of sweet lavender filled the air. Thomas spoke.

"Mrs. Mellor. You're intruding."

Ella opened her eyes in alarm and they confirmed what Thomas had unerringly inferred by sound and scent alone.

Blackheath Manor's housekeeper stared at them with a thunderous countenance.

Chapter Twenty-One

Dear Ella, I cannot thank you enough for the surprise gift of sheet music last month. What a talent you have uncovered in Mr. Thomas Searle.

The Bishop and I are greatly surprised we have not heard his name before, but we so rarely get to Bedfordshire and, as you mention, he has not yet embarked on his career.

The Bishop is rather taken with the notion of being a patron of the arts in what small way he can, so he has instructed me to ask whether Mr. Searle would consider a paid commission to turn his Cantata for piano into a full choral piece for the fourth Sunday after Easter.

You have indicated the young man is shy, but we would count it a great blessing if he were to play the piano himself with the cathedral choir. In any event, please do pass on my admiration of his clear talent, (but you may omit my confession that, on first playing his work, I was nearly overcome with emotion!).

God bless you, and with sincere regards,
Prudence Stanton.

Ella was delighted at Mrs Stanton's response to the samples of Thomas's music. She only hoped the publishers in London to whom she had sent a full parcel would feel the same way. She carried the letter in her pocket, waiting until she could share it with Thomas.

This was the night of the Blackheath Manor summer party.

The house and grounds were a hive of activity and Ella was glad of a brief respite from it, but she did not tarry in Dunstable, as she might do on her day off. The driver and trap waited for her by the green.

An air of expectation filled her stomach with butterflies as the manor house loomed into view. How could she have thought Blackheath was a bleak and gloomy place? Everything was bright, the red clay bricks and white painted trimmings set to perfection on the luscious green lawn, around which were gardens, dotted with blooming flowers in every color of the rainbow.

Large billowing clouds in pristine white adorned the cerulean sky. Ella breathed in the sweet August air and raised her face to let the sunlight warm her cheeks for a moment before dashing into the cool of the house.

To her right, the double doors to the entrance hall were open wide. At the far end, in front of the now dormant fireplace, a small orchestra was setting up. The piano from the drawing room had been wheeled across for the occasion.

In the nursery on the second floor, Louisa and Grace napped despite their protestations at lunch time. Ella decided to let them sleep for another hour after which they would rehearse, have their dinner and get ready for the party – Louisa in pink and Grace in yellow.

On the first floor, doors which were usually closed were now wide open along with the windows. Inside, maids dusted and prepared bedding for guests planning to stay overnight. Even the schoolroom had been turned into a dormitory with pallets laid for visiting ladies' maids.

At the end of the passage, the sound rising up the servant's staircase from the floors below was a cacophony. Ella paused to catch her breath and knocked at the door on her right.

"Enter!"

She opened the door and had eyes only for Thomas who sat at a table by the window, eating lunch.

"Miss Montgomery! It's most improper that you should be here."

Ella halted at Mrs. Mellor's censure.

"It's alright, Melly," Thomas answered. "Miss Montgomery and I are engaged, after all."

"Not publicly," the older woman countered. "Not until after tonight."

Thomas dipped his head to acknowledge the rightness of her statement. He dabbed his mouth with the napkin and dropped in on the table.

"And these are exceptional circumstances."

He turned to Ella expectantly, his voice unable to disguise hope. "Any news?"

"Nothing from the publishers yet, but I *do* have this."

Ella reached into her pocket and unfolded the letter from Prudence Stanton.

She read it out loud to Thomas and, when she came to the end of it, there was a sob.

Mrs. Mellor touched a handkerchief to her eyes. "Dearest boy, dearest boy... How you've suffered all these years."

The woman's sobs turned to open weeping.

Thomas reached for his stick. The wooden chair legs scraped across the floor as he rose. He put his arm around the woman, her head only just reaching his shoulder. She embraced him tightly.

"Shhh... That's all in the past," he soothed. "Tonight is the beginning of a new future; one which wouldn't have happened without you. Everyone else left me to die, but not you, Melly. You helped me get stronger. You believed in me when I started playing; when I could barely get my left hand working again. My gratitude to you is unending."

Tears slipped down Ella's own face as she silently repented of every unkind thought she had had about the woman, then Mrs. Mellor saw her and drew herself up abruptly.

"Compose yourself, Miss Montgomery," the housekeeper said sharply, dabbing at her own tears. "You cannot set foot in front of guests with red eyes."

The hint of a smile from behind the kerchief took the sting from the woman's stern words.

"Your advice is sage, Mrs. Mellor." Ella said, drying her eyes and smiling at the two people in front of her.

Thomas slapped his free hand on his thigh.

"Come, ladies," he said, a broad smile lighting his features, "this is no time for weeping. There is still work to do before we surprise my dear brother with the debut of Thomas Searle.

Mrs. Mellor composed herself swiftly and walked to the door, then paused. She looked sternly at Ella as she addressed Thomas.

"I will return in ten minutes with one of the footmen to help you dress, Mr. Thomas. I expect you to be alone."

As soon as the door closed, Ella rushed into Thomas' arms. He seemed to kiss her everywhere – her neck, her cheeks, her lips – no part of her face escaped his passion, which was answered in equal measure by her.

"Darling Ella, I'm dreaming. Tell me I'm dreaming."

"You're not, my love. This is very, very real."

Thomas broke their embrace and took a step to the side. He tapped the base of a tall chest of drawers with his stick as if to locate it and cautiously lowered himself onto one knee, touching each knob on the drawers until he found the correct one and pulled it open.

"When Mrs. Mellor says ten minutes, she means it," he said.

He withdrew a small casket inlaid with mother-of-pearl from the drawer, placed it on the floor and opened it. He spent a moment rummaging through before locating what he was searching for. Thomas reached out to Ella, turned over his hand and unfurled his fingers.

"If I've chosen correctly, this is a posy ring which belonged to my grandmother."

In his palm was a little gold ring with seven gemstones – diamond, emerald, amethyst, ruby, another emerald, a sapphire and a topaz – mounted in the shape of a tiny flower.

"I know I have already asked once," he said, looking up to her, "but, Ella Jayne Montgomery, will you accept this as my token and be my wife?"

Ella sank to her knees in front of him and silently placed her left hand in his while wiping fresh tears from her cheek with the other.

Thomas cleared his throat. "You'll have to say the words, my love. It may have escaped your notice, but I'm blind."

Ella giggled and realized she sounded like one of the children. She pulled herself together.

"Thomas James Worsley," she said, seriously, "I accept the honor of becoming your wife and your partner in this adventure to come. I will love you always."

He rose to his feet, keeping her hand in his, and found the third finger of her left hand, slipping the ring on, where it sat perfectly.

They embraced, then Thomas stepped back.

"Let's go through our plans one more time."

Chapter Twenty-Two

Ella squeezed the handkerchief in her pocket. It was Thomas's and she pretended it was his hand she squeezed instead.

The ivory gown she wore was new. It had taken her much time to finish sewing it and it seemed appropriate it would make its debut tonight – like Thomas.

Louisa and Grace sat together on a chair talking nineteen to the dozen, their little stockinged feet peeking out from the hems of their dresses as they swung their legs back and forth.

Ella captured one foot and gave it a tickle before slipping a leather shoe on it. She repeated the process another three times.

"Ready, girls?" she asked. "A deep breath and exhale slowly. It won't do to get too excited."

They descended via the main staircase. Ella glanced at the landing on the first floor then continued down. Thomas would be nearly ready. She was glad she had Louisa and Grace's hands to hold; the action masked the unavoidable shaking of her own.

His plan was audacious. He was betting upon his own skill as a pianist – and his brother's pride.

To unmask Thomas, William would have to denounce himself and risk scandal. This way, Thomas Worsley could remain dead along with his twin brother, and William's social standing as a man of refined tastes would be enhanced with his patronage of a new musical talent.

And, should anyone remark on the family resemblance, Thomas Searle was but a distant cousin.

"Remember girls," said Ella softly, "as we rehearsed."

The Earl and Lady Margaret stood at the receiving line, greeting the last of the guests.

"Bon soir, maman, bon soir, papa," the girls said in unison.

"My darlings, you look splendid," said Lady Margaret, her smile full.

Ella reflected that tonight, in her indigo blue gown, Lady Margaret recalled the wedding portrait – young and carefree. Beside her, William Worsley looked every inch the Earl in a deep green frock coat.

"Perform well tonight, mind. Make your father proud," he commanded.

Louisa and Grace nodded, but their eyes were already focused on the room filled with beautifully dressed men and women.

"Ready?" Ella whispered to them.

They moved through the room; the Earl and the Countess followed behind. The hubbub of conversation dropped as they passed and a few of the guests remarked how pretty the girls were, how much they had grown, how much alike they had become– so much like their father in coloring.

Ella helped Grace, then Louisa onto the piano stool together and waited for them to ready themselves. Ella tapped a count with a finger and Louisa started with the first note of Greensleeves, which they played as a duet, followed by Frere Jacque with Ella as the third voice and accompanying them on the piano.

The twins' performance of their two pieces was nearly flawless and met with polite applause.

"Ladies and gentlemen," Ella announced, "the Ladies Louisa and Grace Worsley would like to thank you for listening to their performance tonight."

The girls curtsied to their audience, eliciting another smattering of applause before Ella instructed them to go to Mrs. Mellor who waited near the servants' door by the orchestra. Behind her, over the voices of guests who had begun to talk again, she heard the familiar tapping of Thomas's stick and knew that beside him would be a footman to guide him along tonight's unfamiliar path to the piano.

Ella glanced at the Earl. His face paled as he recognized his brother emerging from the door by which Mrs. Mellor stood. Then Ella took a deep breath and, rising from the piano stool, spoke the words she had rehearsed with Thomas.

"Ladies and gentlemen, I have been asked to announce an unscheduled entertainment. Making his concert debut tonight is a man of rare talent – Mr. Thomas Searle."

She slipped out from behind the stool, letting Thomas in, and he held out his stick for her to take before sitting down. Ella stood by Mrs Mellor and the girls.

For a moment, he sat with his head bowed over the keyboard, unmoving, as though in prayer. The hubbub around the room decreased to silence. Ella held her breath and looked again at the Earl.

William's face had turned from pale to puce. He took a step forward but Lady Margaret laid a hand on his shoulder.

Thomas played the first notes of a Fugue from Bach. The set of his jaw was a testament to his concentration. The piece started slowly with one hand. Those who did not recognize the tune started to murmur. Then they stopped. The atmosphere was charged throughout the four minutes in which Thomas dominated the complex piece.

At the end, there was a bright burst of applause which Thomas immediately silenced with the beginning of another piece. It was a nocturne of his own creation – light and ethereal, a contrast to the intensity of the Bach.

Thomas played the final note and let it fade. With a hand on the fallboard, he pushed himself up to a standing position, turned to the room and bowed briefly from the waist. Then he remained with his head lowered – a man awaiting a jury's verdict. Would he be vindicated or condemned?

Ella clutched the handkerchief in her pocket. She could feel her knuckles ache. Then it happened.

Loud applause and even cheers crashed down like waves on the shore. Although Thomas's head remained bowed, Ella could see a broad smile emerging with the ever more demanding calls for an encore.

Thomas finally stood upright, allowing everyone to see his scarred face fully, but the applause never faltered. He stretched out his right arm out and turned his face in Ella's direction.

This was not rehearsed.

Ella stepped forward and took Thomas's hand. He drew her near, then held up his left hand for silence.

"Thank you for your kind reception of my first recital. I would like to thank the Earl of Renthorpe for his benevolence in permitting me to perform for you tonight."

"Where is William?" Thomas murmured aside to Ella.

"To your left."

Thomas bowed in his brother's direction as another call of 'encore' rose from here and there.

"No, you are too kind," responded Thomas, "and I would not outstay my welcome. But I feel compelled to share with you that this is a doubly happy occasion because I've persuaded Miss Montgomery here to become my wife."

Beneath polite applause from the guests, Thomas whispered: "How does William look?"

"Apoplectic."

"I'm not surprised."

"And he's coming towards us; slowly though – people are congratulating him."

"And Margaret?"

Ella looked again and her eyes met Lady Margaret's. Of any, she was the one Ella most regretted deceiving in this way, but her set face betrayed nothing. Then she glanced at her husband as if to assure herself she wasn't observed, and mouthed the word 'bravo' across the room to Ella.

"I think Lady Margaret is pleased," Ella whispered to Thomas as his brother finally arrived within arm's distance and the orchestra struck up behind them.

"*Mister* Searle, is it?" said William, taking Thomas's hand in his in the pretence of shaking it.

"*Cousin*, if you prefer."

William leaned in close, the odor of brandy already strong enough on his breath that Ella could smell it.

"You were supposed to stay dead."

For a moment, it seemed the Earl had forgotten Thomas was blind and could not be quailed by fierce expression. But Ella could see William's face and, when it turned to her, she could not help the tremor that ran through her at his thunderous glare.

"And as for you, you deceitful little trollop–"

His words ceased abruptly to Ella's confusion before she realized the Earl's right hand was still in Thomas's and was being crushed in a powerful grasp.

"Watch how you speak to my fiancée, William," he cautioned, then released his brother's hand.

"Do you think to embarrass me, Thomas?" demanded William, rubbing his strained fingers.

"On the contrary. I seek to release you.

"Tonight I am resurrected as either Thomas Searle, a distant cousin, or Thomas Worsley, your elder brother and rightful heir to Renthorpe.

"I'm emerging from the grave, William.

"Which person am I to be?"

Epilogue

"Stop pacing," said Thomas, "you're making me nervous." Ella halted. He was nervous? *She* was nervous. Today marked the debut of the full choral cantata Bishop Stanton had commissioned.

She took a deep breath and peered out at the growing crowd taking their places on the pews in the nave. In the crossing, where the nave intersected with the north and south transept, the orchestra tuned up. She closed the door and turned back to her husband.

Thomas, dressed formally in black, sat on a straight backed chair in a little room off the presbytery in the magnificent Lincoln Cathedral. He rolled his walking stick in both hands. This particular one was new – ebony with a silver terminal, a gift from Lady Margaret who was in the audience today, along with Louisa and Grace.

Her husband. Ella's heart swelled at the fact.

She observed him now, wishing she could deal with her anxiety as masterfully as he dealt with his. Thomas's eyes were closed in meditation – a quiet ritual she had come to know of him this past eight months. He would remain seated with his eyes closed until it was time to perform.

Ella sat on the seat opposite Thomas and closed her eyes too. Perhaps it would help.

She breathed deeply and thought on all that had happened after that fateful night the previous August...

The door of the solicitor's office had opened and Thomas walked out.

"Ready to go?" he asked.

She took his arm and escorted him down the main stairs of the chambers to a waiting carriage.

Ella couldn't wait any longer.

"Well?"

The conveyance had jolted, pushing them closer together.

"Very civilized, all things considered. William and I have come to terms – for my renouncement of any future claim by myself and my heirs, he will sign over the deeds to the townhouse in London and restore the income from my grandmother's estate that should have been mine by rights. It's not an extravagant income, but enough to keep house and buy some time enough to start earning a living."

Thomas brought her fingers to his lips.

"Any regrets, my love, at leaving Blackheath Manor to marry a penniless musician?"

"None at all," she assured him.

"Ah! So *if music be the food of love, play on*?"

"Oh no, I'm much more practical than that, sir. Here."

Ella placed a paper in his hand and watched Thomas run a finger over the edge of the rectangular document.

"What is it?"

"It's a bank note. A *twenty pound* bank note."

"Where did this amount of money come from?"

"From your *publisher*."

He laughed.

"You'd best take this away from me before it slips through my fingers."

Ella took the note and put it securely in her reticule.

"Since when do I have a publisher?"

"Since this morning when I went to check the post office in Dunstable. It was sent by recorded post. They were full of praise of the first suite of music and they say they are eager to receive the second parcel. They want to meet you."

Thomas hollered loudly, startling the horse momentarily so it broke pace. The coachman had looked back askance at them, but they hadn't cared. The pure joy on Thomas's face filled her heart with more love than Ella thought she was ever capable of feeling.

Then he kissed her over and over again...

Ella smiled at the memory of that day. And now, every day, they created new memories together, each one happier than the last.

"Are you ready?" a man's voice gently enquired. Ella opened her eyes to Bishop Stanton, dressed in Easter vestments of pure white with the wide gold embroidered ribbon across the yoke and down the centre, a pattern repeated on his miter.

Thomas stood and the bishop took his hand warmly and offered his blessing before Ella stepped forward. Today, she was dressed in the finest gown she owned – her wedding dress of apricot silk. The sound of it rustled as she approached and Thomas, hearing it, held out his hand for her to take.

She threaded her fingers through his and he gave it a comforting squeeze. Ella touched her other hand to his elbow and they moved out of the room.

She escorted Thomas to the piano amid polite applause at his entrance, and waited for him to orient himself. He bowed in the direction of the distinguished guests, whose location he knew from rehearsals, and then to the audience.

"There are a lot of people here," said Thomas quietly.

"They will love you as I love you," she assured him.

"I hope that's not *quite* true," he smiled mischievously.

Ella took her place beside the Bishop and his wife, and the choir master tapped his baton, calling for silence.

She held her breath. The atmosphere was charged. Thomas's hands descended and he played the opening bars with passion.

Ella exhaled slowly and closed her eyes to listen. It seemed more fitting this way.

Critics were praising his works and audiences gave rapturous applause.

But no matter how large an audience Thomas now played to, she would always remember the dark nights at Blackheath Manor when he played for her alone.

THE END

SEPTEMBER HARVEST

Tilly is twelve years old when seasonal crop picker Andrew,
still just a boy himself, introduces her to reading.

Instantly besotted both with Andrew and with books,
Tilly eagerly awaits his return to her village
over the course of six summers.

Childish adoration is now a young woman's love but has she
misread his feelings for her over the years?

A sensitive picture of life and growing up in rural Kent
in the late 1800s.

September Harvest

The whole world was yellow, the sun's long afternoon rays bathing the village ahead in golden light.

Tilly turned away from her lengthening shadow and looked back towards the setting sun. It threw the landscape into such stark relief against the rich blue of the sky that she felt her eyes hurt with the sharpness of it.

But it was a trick. The light wasn't warm like the midday sun – rather it was cold, like the gold coin she had once held briefly in her hand.

Neatly planted rows of hops reached for the sky, the tendrils of the vines reaching heavenward to wave in the breeze, as though bidding goodbye to the sun for another day.

The sun responded by blowing rosy-tinged kisses as the sky's blue faded, the wind freshened and the last of the glowing orb disappeared over the hill that separated this village from the rugged Kent coastline beyond.

Still Tilly lingered at the crossroads separating the fields from the edge of the village and the tavern which was her home.

She drew a hand over light brown hair to remove the curly strands from her eyes and watched the rose sky turn purple.

Out of the corner of her eye she saw the first of the evening stars wink into view and she wondered, as she had done on this eve so many times before, whether he saw it too.

They would be here soon, within days, the workers to help with the harvest. They would come from the outlying towns and villages – even, as she well knew, from as far away as London. They would pull down the bines on which the hops vines grew and everyone – children included – would walk through the yards picking the cones to be taken to the nearby oast houses for drying and brewing into beer drunk the length and breadth of Britain.

Tilly wondered whether Andrew would return. At the thought, her heart tumbled several hollow beats.

She pulled her rough woollen shawl over her shoulders and turned back to the tavern. Whitewashed walls glowed in what was left of the light as she approached and opened the oak door, black with age.

It gave way to the kitchen and inside, the glow was more orange than gold from the large fire that warmed the flagstone-floored room. Cut wood sufficient for the evening and the next morning had been stacked to the side of the hearth by Noah. From the tavern, above a hubbub of voices, she could hear Gwen calling for Agnes to clear the tables.

Tilly stepped inside and closed the door firmly to keep in the heat. An apron hung by a peg at the door and she put it on, tying the long white strips of fabric neatly behind her.

As she started her evening chores, Tilly allowed her mind to wander back to another September day, seven summers earlier.

Andrew was little more than a boy himself, just fifteen, when she first laid eyes on him, and she was only twelve.

* * *

She offered the boy a shy smile as she dropped the bounty from her apron onto the clean sack spread on the ground – hard yellow cheeses, crisp red apples and loaves of freshly baked bread still warm from the oven.

"I thought you might be hungry," she said to them generally but looking at him as she spoke.

He lounged in the shade, sweat glistening on his skin, his black hair damp and slicked to his face from the morning's work. His body was that of a youth, although he did the work of a man.

"Send 'er packin', Andrew," said one of the other lads who rested with him, reaching for an apple. "Tell 'er to come back with ale next time."

"Yeah," chimed in a third, a particularly mean looking boy, skinny with red hair, face and arms heavily freckled. Tilly didn't like Reggie. He threw rocks at her when the other boys weren't watching.

But two weeks gone, Andrew caught Reggie throwing stones and making her cry, and he clipped the red-haired boy briskly across the side of the head, chiding him.

From that moment on, Andrew was Tilly's hero.

Now, he ignored his companions and greeted her with a smile.

"What light from yonder window breaks, it is the east and Juliet is the sun..."

Tilly had flushed, although she had no idea what he meant, but then he was always reading something in those books.

The other boy, Nathaniel, groaned loud and long. "Give it a rest, will ye. No one cares that ye can read and write – fat lot of good it'll do ye labouring in the fields."

Tilly felt her face flare redder still, but now with righteous anger at Nathaniel's disdain towards Andrew.

"Take that back! It were mean!" she cried.

Nathaniel's expression, at first astonished, turned to amused in a scant second.

"Don't listen to them, Andrew," she begged over the snorts of laughter. "You can read all you want to. You can read to *me*."

Salty, bitter tears fringed the corner of her vision, but she was determined not to let them fall.

Andrew looked at her, not mocking like the other boys did, but with a soft, almost dreamy expression in those warm brown eyes.

"Thank you, Tilly."

He spoke her name softly and she was sure she didn't imagine the special appreciation in his eyes. And, when she was out of sight, her slow walk turned to a skip, her mood buoyed by his notice of her which lasted until the end of the day.

Over the remainder of that week, she noticed he spent less time with the other boys during the periods of rest, and instead would be sitting on his own, his attention riveted to the small red volume he brought from his pocket.

A few days after that, she shyly approached him again, asking if he would read to her. And he did!

It was a story by a man called Alexandre Dumas. And she hung on to every word, transported to a world far away from the heat and the hard work of the harvest. Every night, she would recall the words and Andrew's voice and the smiles he would give her as he shared the adventure that existed within the pages of his little red volume of *The Count Of Monte Cristo*.

A magical September finally drew to a close, and the workers left one by one, family by family. The harvest was complete and the last of the hops cones had been spread out in the vast oast houses.

It was Andrew's turn to leave, to return to London where Tilly had learned his widowed mother lived. She tried not to cry when he clambered up on to the dray that would take the last of the pickers north for a few miles before they would have to make the rest of their way back on foot.

She would miss him and was doubly sad because now she would never know if Dantes survived being thrown into the sea. Her future seemed as uncertain as that of the hero of the book.

The dozen men and women on the dray waved farewell to the villagers and Tilly absently raised her own hand in response.

"Hey-up!" called the driver and the sturdy draught horse stepped forward, hooves stirring up dust that clouded its pale fetlocks.

Tilly saw Andrew glance about as though looking for something, then his eyes lit on hers. He bounded off the moving cart and ran back to her.

She found the slim red volume in her hands.

"Read it. The ending. Keep it safe for me until next year."

She nodded but no words were possible before he turned in pursuit of the cart and leapt back on board. She felt the trickle of a tear roll down her face and clutched the precious volume to her chest.

When the cart disappeared out of sight, she ran and hid and wept bitter tears, stopping only when the voice of her father called her back to her chores.

* * *

Tilly could not help but smile at the memory of that first year and, in her mind's eye, she could still see the red covered book and recall the feel of the stiff card binding, the soft thickness of the paper, and the crisply printed words that opened up a world of magic far beyond the quiet borders of her village in Kent.

Until the moment Andrew pressed the book into her hands, she had had little interest in mastering the art of reading beyond what little she had learned at school, but now applied herself to the task ferociously and, for the entire year, kept the precious little volume safe under her pillow.

Slowly and laboriously at first, she read it from cover to cover. Then, getting used to the words, she read it over again until once more the summer blossomed in all its glory.

When the sweet smell from the neighbouring apple orchards heralded the arrival of autumn, she kissed the little volume for the last time and anticipated returning it to its owner when he arrived with the rest of the labourers.

* * *

Tilly rolled out the pastry and dropped it deftly in the dish. She spooned macerated blueberries into the pastry, covered the pie with another piece of rolled out dough and decorated the lid with the remnants, little round discs resembling the fruit contained within.

For a moment, she listened to the noises of the night's customers in the pub. The ladies from the Temperance League would not approve, she thought wryly as she opened the door on the stove and slid the dish in.

But hopefully they *would* approve of the proper coffee house next door. They didn't need to know the same kitchen provided for *both* establishments. The coffee house opened at breakfast and closed not long after nightfall, after which the public house continued its trade.

She had run the public house herself since her father died last year when she was barely seventeen. He had been the Red Lion's publican as his father had been before him and Tilly was to be when she attained her full age.

The coffee house was a recent addition however, an idea she'd had to recoup income lost to the Temperance ladies' efforts in the church.

More and more frequently, Tilly found herself fending off the attentions of would-be suitors, often much older than she, men in their thirties, even forties, who had more of an eye for the income brought in by the pub than any real regard for her.

To that end, Noah's constant presence had been a blessing – helpful, undemanding and familiar. He frequently helped out around the tavern though his real work was as one of the junior foremen at the oast house.

Tilly had known him since infancy and she supposed that few knew her traits as thoroughly. But Noah, sweet as he was, could never *understand* her as Andrew did. Perhaps no man could.

Tilly took in a deep breath to sigh, and the sweet notes of the blueberry pie baking mingled with rich aroma of the oxtail stew being served up as tonight's dinner.

She looked up at the sound of Agnes bustling into the kitchen with an armload of dirty dishes.

"Ah, you're back, miss," said the serving girl.

The note of relief in the thirteen year old's voice didn't escape notice, or that the child's round, rosy cheeks were even more flushed than usual. It must be an especially busy night out in the dining room, thought Tilly.

"I am," she smiled, remembering herself at that age. Over the clattering dishes in the tub, Tilly called, "Get along home now, Agnes, and don't forget to take a loaf and some stew."

She watched the girl ladle a generous helping of the food into a tin bucket. The gentle tendrils of steam were like an escaping genie captured with a firm press of the lid. Tilly waited a moment before speaking again.

"How is your reading coming along?"

Agnes pulled a face momentarily and mumbled under her breath.

"You know that was the condition when I gave you this job, Agnes," Tilly reminded her firmly. "You can work here and take food home to your brothers on the condition you learn to read and write."

"I'm grateful Miss Tilly, truly I am, but it's... *borin'*" she replied, keeping her gaze fixed resolutely to the floor.

"You find Alice in Wonderland boring?"

Agnes shrugged.

"Even the talking cat?"

The girl looked up for a split second then back to the floor but Tilly had seen the girl's wide eyes flash with surprised excitement and they confirmed her suspicions. Agnes had not gone beyond the first chapter, perhaps not even the first page.

"I shall make you a bargain," said Tilly, and Agnes's head raised slightly with as much curiosity as suspicion. "You read one chapter a week, and tell the story back to me as we work in the kitchen, and you can take a fruit pie home too. Just a small one, mind. Could you do that?"

Agnes nodded her dirty blonde head quickly. "Ooh, yes, Miss Tilly," she said, gathering her things and heading out into the quickening twilight.

As the door slammed behind Agnes, Tilly pondered for a moment whether it was the attraction of a talking cat or a fruit pie that earned the girl's quick assent to the deal. She turned back to her work, deep in thought.

Even though all children were supposed to attend school until the age of thirteen, not everyone was able to take advantage of Mr. Gladstone's education bill. Girls like Agnes had family responsibilities and, far away from the watchful social reformers in the city, were not pursued if they missed classes.

Tilly offered a resigned shake of her head to the four walls. She remembered what it was like to have little schooling and even less opportunity to learn, so no matter what this September brought, she would be forever grateful to Andrew introducing her to books.

Andrew...

When she was Agnes's age, she thought he was the sun, the moon and the stars. She allowed herself a wistful smile as she walked into the dining room to assist old Gwen who was working behind the bar.

Tilly wiped down the tables and cleared tankards and empty bottles, acknowledging the regulars drinking quietly over the draughts boards or playing table skittles.

Noah was there too, sitting with the men from other farms, dusty and sweat-stained after a long day's work. The others continued their talk, heedless of her, but Noah watched her, brushing a lock of sandy hair out of his eyes.

She acknowledged his glance with a smile. He nodded once and returned to the conversation.

* * *

In her fourteenth year, Andrew brought *Mill On The Floss*. They had taken turns reading aloud during the noontime breaks in the sunshine.

On Sundays after church, when the labourers and villagers gathered on the green to play cricket, she and Andrew would walk down into the woods to find the stream that flowed through it, discussing whether Tom was right to end Maggie and Phillip's relationship.

The following year it was *Oliver Twist*. The next, *Emma*. And it was in that year she was certain she loved him.

Andrew was twenty then, very nearly a man, and beginning to show signs of a man's physique. His shoulders had broadened and the gangly youth was gone – replaced by a maturity that was attracting more than the occasional admiring eye from other girls.

And yet he spent most of his free time with her. Tilly had felt pride at that, and a growing confidence he thought of her as more than just a reading companion.

One night, to celebrate the end of the harvest season, she had been allowed to attend her first dance in the company of her friend Peggy and Peggy's parents. The harvest dance was the biggest dance of the year, attended by all the villagers and the workers.

Tilly had worn her best dress, soft violet in hue, and it clung gently to her figure, reminding anyone watching that she was now a young woman, no longer a child. When she stepped out into the small little parlour, her father stood by the fire, his arm resting on the mantle. He took her in from head to toe, then pulled the pipe from his mouth. Wisps of blue-grey smoke rose as he breathed out.

"'Tis my regret your ma isn't here to see you now, all growed up," he said, then his expression became stern. "You be mindful of the boys, don't be stepping outside with them. Don't be bringin' disgrace on this house, you hear?"

Tilly swore solemnly she would not, but – though it mattered deeply to her – it wasn't her father's approval she sought this night.

From the moment she arrived at the dance, Tilly searched the crowd looking for Andrew. Then she found him, there in one of the concentric circles of dancers. She watched him move anticlockwise along with the other men, proud of how handsome he looked and how smart he was in his Sunday clothes.

The dance was coming to an end and the men and women who had not yet danced, readied themselves. Tilly stood and made her way to the refreshments table where she guessed Andrew would go.

Her skin tingled as the crowd about the table thickened. He was behind her, sure of it despite the press of the crowd.

"Excuse me, miss," he said as he edged beside to accept a cup. Tilly paused with her own cup in hand and waited for him to turn. He did and his eyes widened and her heart swelled under his scrutiny.

"What happened to the little girl who always follows me around?" he asked and she was delighted to hear the question was slightly breathless.

"She's all grown up, sir."

"Yes, I can see that."

Tilly's smile widened and she dropped a small curtsey but her good humour ebbed as Nathaniel and Reggie joined them.

"We're heading outside for something more stimulating than punch if you know what I mean," said

Nathaniel, surreptitiously showing a small earthenware cider flask grasped beneath his coat.

Tilly still couldn't bring herself to like Andrew's friends. At least they didn't pick on her like they used to – they were too busy flirting with the girls in the field to pay attention to her – and she was glad for that.

Now Reggie eyed her with distinct male appreciation. Tilly took a step backwards as though his look were a touch. She turned to Andrew in silent appeal. Did he recognise it too?

He must have done because his expression hardened a moment.

"Miss Tilly, will you save me at least one dance?"

His expression may have clouded over but, for Tilly, it was as though summer sunlight filled her.

"I will indeed, sir," she smiled in what she hoped was sophisticated flirtatiousness before looking to those now dancing. "That is, as long as my dance card is not already filled."

* * *

It was a grand evening with no shortage of dance partners and friendly girls to gossip with, though not everyone danced, she observed. Noah and his friends from the village were dull; they never danced.

Tilly, however, threw herself into both dance and gossip with gusto and it almost came as a surprise when Andrew finally came to claim his appointment.

She smiled at him but he only made a half-hearted attempt to smile back as he offered her his hand. Tilly took it and his warm, firm fingers closed over hers. She felt as though she could float away on the sensation.

Couples lined up in a row for a long ways dance and Andrew's claim on her hand strengthened as the dancers prepared to step forward.

As they turned, his hand touched her waist. Tilly felt a strange sensation course through her, radiating from his hand upon her. It made her feel breathless. She turned her gaze up to him and watched his face, dear and familiar to her after so many harvests. He wore an expression she could not recall seeing before.

Then the dance was over and the music stopped, but her heart couldn't stop beating with it, leaving her breathless.

"Do you want to sit down?" he asked in concern.

Tilly shook her head. Andrew still held her hand and she did not want him to stop.

"Perhaps some fresh air outside would be better. You look all flushed."

She nodded, forgetting her father's admonishment, and Andrew took her out into the cool night air where the trees cast deep twilight shadows across the green. They stayed within sight of the church hall and sat on a bench in the semi-darkness with the sounds of crickets and the nightingales competing with the merry sound of the fiddlers.

Andrew removed his jacket and Tilly could feel his heat in it, then sensed the smell of lemon soap and its weight as he pressed it on her shoulders. The strange sensation she had experienced during the dance came back.

"I thought you might be getting chilled," Andrew said, his voice muted, his tone strange.

Was something wrong? Tilly licked her lips and drew breath to ask but was stopped as Andrew lowered his mouth to hers.

Those lips were soft, so much softer than his hard, working hands. It was the first time Tilly had been kissed and she wondered whether it was possible to die from the sensation.

She moved closer to him and his arms encircled her. His mouth coaxed hers open and the kisses deepened.

And stopped.

Tilly opened her eyes and saw Andrew as breathless as herself. Her ears buzzed as though she stood in the middle of a sun-kissed wildflower meadow full of bees, her skin tingled from the same invisible glow of sunlight.

"I shouldn't have done that," he said, although it seemed to her he muttered it more to himself than her. Tilly was too breathless to ask why.

He stood and gently drew her to her feet.

"We'd better get back inside before you're missed."

Tilly raised no protest and kept pace with him but the magic of the moment was gone. Now all she felt was the damp evening air numbing her even beneath Andrew's jacket.

But he kissed her! Andrew kissed her … then regretted it.

It was the best and worst night ever.

They reached the edge of where the lamplight would touch them and he slowed his pace, then stopped.

She looked up at him and saw the same expression he had right before he kissed her. He raised a hand and his touch felt cool against her cheek. Work-roughened fingers stroked her skin. Her eyes shuttered closed and his thumb brushed against her lips which parted of their own accord.

"Tilly, you've grown up so pretty," he whispered. "I wish..."

She opened her eyes and beheld the longing in Andrew's own as he lowered his hand.

His name was the only word capable of leaving her lips so she had said it softly, reverently.

"Save me another dance?" he asked.

She readily nodded, returning his jacket, and he took her arm in his – like a gentleman would for a lady – and escorted her back into the hall.

* * *

A loud yawn interrupted Tilly's recollection. She looked up to see Gwen covering her mouth with the back of her hand.

"Ring the bell, Gwen," Tilly told her and the older woman shot her a look of gratitude. As Gwen rang for last orders, Tilly returned to the kitchen to take out the freshly baked pie. It would join the other coffee house pastries she'd made today.

As she set the pie to cool, her fingers accidentally brushed against the hot metal dish and the vestiges of her September harvest memories scattered. She shook her hand to ease the momentary pain and made her way back into the pub.

"Time, gentlemen!" she called and joined Gwen behind the bar, bringing a small tub of hot soapy water to tackle the small mountain of dirty vessels that waited.

She nudged her old friend gently with her shoulder as she settled the tub on the bench. "Go on, head off for bed. You have to open the coffee shop tomorrow."

"What about those two?"

Tilly smiled at the last two patrons – two elderly gentlemen, both stooped and grey, peering with great concentration at the draughtsboard, their pewter pots no doubt still a quarter full. She knew the routine. Now she had called closing, they would make their final drinks linger as long as possible. Tilly raised her voice slightly to answer Gwen, just to be sure the two men heard her.

"Mr. Beasley and Mr. Perkins have until I finish washing these glasses before I toss them out."

Mr. Perkins raised a vague hand in acknowledgement. Tilly smiled at the familiar ruse. Then his features animated and Tilly heard the crisp sound of clip, clip, clip, clip, clop as a black roundel of timber zig-zagged across the board. Mr. Beasley sighed his disappointment at being at the losing end of the game.

Soon the chores were done and the wall clock chimed the eleventh hour. The two elderly gentlemen shuffled their way out the door, wishing her a good night. They would be back again tomorrow night – they were here every night except Sunday when the tavern was closed.

The rasp of the bolt sliding home on the front door sounded loudly, then it was silent except for the occasional pop and hiss of the low-banked fire in the room and the steady, ever-present tick of the clock. With the premises locked and secure, her own bed waited for her. Gwen had thoughtfully lit a lamp and placed it on the pot cupboard. Tilly undressed by it and climbed into the bed which had once been her parents'.

She turned to extinguish the light and her eyes fell across the volume of *Emma*.

The memory of the kiss lingered. Tilly allowed herself a small smile at the thought of it – nearly two years ago now, slightly faded with time, like the forget-me-not she pressed between the final unprinted page and the back cover. Both the kiss and the book were kept as private mementoes of that September.

* * *

Andrew's departure had been the same as every other year, but this time, as he pressed the copy of *Emma* into her hands, he whispered, "Keep it."

It sustained her through the bleak winter of that year, the one that claimed her father with pneumonia. He died late February, just three days after Tilly's seventeenth birthday. He was buried in the winter church yard and the cold hard earth was softened, at least to look at, by the sprinkling of snow as the villagers pressed in close, as much for mutual warmth as comfort on that desolate, cloud-filled morning.

The tavern was bequeathed to her and, despite her youth, Tilly was allowed to run it as she wished, so long as she remained a person of good character. The licence was held in trust by the parish council. Gwen, being a respectable widow, was charged with her guardianship until Tilly attained her full age.

The older woman moved into the home in the back of the tavern and, though also charged with guiding Tilly's management of the pub, saw enough maturity in her to defer to her judgement in running the establishment.

On Tilly's part, she had been glad of the company – and an additional and willing pair of hands to help.

And once more the days lengthened and grew warm, though the chill of grief and loss around her heart lingered.

* * *

Tilly extinguished the lamp.

As she waited for sleep to claim her, memories of the kiss gave way inescapably to thoughts of the subsequent September and Tilly recalled it with shame and regret, grateful that only the darkness could see.

If her sixteenth year had been the best of her life, her seventeenth had been the worst.

* * *

Last September, for the first time in her recollection, Tilly could not be there for the arrival of the seasonal workers. Too busy for that, or to go out into the fields daily as she had done when her father was alive, she had employed Agnes, one of the village girls, to deliver lunch to the workers.

It was a full week into the harvest, and she had yet to see Andrew and little time to consider that he had not come to seek her out either.

Perhaps he hadn't come this year. Panic had stuttered through her at the thought. He *had* to come! She needed him; she had waited all year to see him again.

Tilly got her chance when a group of Temperance ladies from the parish decided to adopt an idea sweeping the larger towns and cities. News arrived one afternoon that they were setting up a temporary 'coffee palace' in the church hall, in the hope that the dark, rich aroma of freshly ground coffee beans would tempt customers away from the tavern at day's end.

Under the pretence of getting a closer look at the 'competition', Tilly went to the church hall, then slipped away to the harvest fields.

Many of the bines were already down across the first quarter of the field and women sat on the ground passing them hand over hand, checking each sinuous strand to catch every cone. Children clustered around huge baskets, stripping away remaining leaves before men came to hoist the bounty onto their shoulders and deposit their burden onto the drays.

Tilly didn't see Andrew among the workers, so she walked up and down between the solid walls of hops supported on props of timber thirty feet tall and threaded with string. She glanced up into the azure late afternoon sky where grassy green bines fluttered in the breeze like pennants.

The unease she felt earlier evaporated under such a beautiful day. He was here, she knew it. They would fall into welcome familiarity. She would tell Andrew everything that had happened over the past year and he would tell her how his mother fared, about his studies to be a teacher but, more importantly, Andrew would tell her how much he missed her and ...

"Well, hello there. I thought I dreamed last September but here you are, all grown up."

Her woolgathering came to an abrupt end but it was not Andrew who spoke. Before Tilly stood Nathaniel, stripped to the waist, the fallen bines behind him blocking her way forward. He too had grown up in all the years he had been coming to Kent from his East London home, but instead as the gentleman Andrew had become, Nathaniel had just grown mean.

"Hello," she responded without enthusiasm. She endured his slow examination of her from head to toe with equanimity. "Have you seen Andrew?"

"Now why are you in such an 'urry to see Andrew? Ain't I good enough for ye?"

Nathaniel stepped towards her. A glint where the sun touched steel drawing her attention to the cutting knife he held in his hand.

Tilly crossed her arms and placed her weight on one hip. If he was going to be an idiot, she was going to be stubborn.

"Do you know where he is or not?"

He pointed the blade across his body. "'Bout a dozen rows down that way, I reckon. He's a bit slower this year because of his girl."

Tilly felt herself frown, and the broader Nathaniel's grin grew, the more she frowned.

"What girl?"

"Ah, ye don't know what happens far away from here when we're gone eleven month of the year, do ye? Well, Andrew's got a girl and now they're gettin' serious he's brought her here with him for the 'arvest."

An unfamiliar tightening of the chest caused Tilly to draw in a deep breath "You're lying," she accused.

"Find out for yourself," he shrugged. "I don't care. I'll be here if you're looking for a manly shoulder to cry on."

A smile, nearly indistinguishable from a sneer, broke across his features and she turned tail and ran, his laughter chasing her down row after row until she spotted Andrew hauling down a section of vine. She picked up her soft blue and cream striped skirts and ran faster.

He turned at the sound of his name and mustered the beginning of a grin before she threw herself at him. She could feel the damp soft cotton of his shirt under her fingers and she held on tight as he spun her about.

"Tilly! I thought you'd gone and got yourself married or something."

She pulled away as he dropped her back to the ground.

"Why would you think that?"

"Well, you weren't here to greet me with the others last week and you seemed all grown up last year, I thought perhaps your father had—"

"—my father died in February."

Andrew blinked rapidly.

"Oh, I'm so sorry." Then he crushed her to him, enveloping her in his arms, one hand cradling her head while the other stroked her back slowly.

"Why didn't you write to me? Why didn't you let me know?"

"I... I... wouldn't know where to address it."

She inhaled the smell of his sweat mingled with the tang of lemon soap and Tilly, all thought of Nathaniel's taunts about another girl gone from her mind, was transported back to the previous September night, her lips tingling in memory of the kiss.

The press of his body against hers awakened something surprising, unfamiliar to her, but she instinctively knew it had something to do with the kiss.

She blinked away tears and when she could see clearly once more, she could tell he remembered too. His head lowered an inch and stopped. As he started to raise it, Tilly stood on the balls of her feet to fill the gap.

The kiss and embrace was as she remembered, an utter contradiction – soft lips and hard muscles, warm mouth and cool breeze at her back.

"Tilly, you don't know what you do to me." His urgent, almost pained whisper answered something deep within. Then there was more, his lips coaxed hers open.

Then she knew he wanted her, needed her, loved her, and she gave everything in return in that kiss.

Then he held her away from him. Tilly frowned not knowing the reason why. Andrew's eyes widened as though alarmed and he scrubbed his hand over his face. She couldn't fathom the reason until the blood rushing in her ears stopped and she heard a female voice, young, perhaps her own age...

"Andy?" the voice called.

Andrew's mouth lost its sensuous softness, and a muscle in his jaw worked slightly.

"Andy? My hands..."

Then from around the end of one of the rows appeared not a girl but a young woman with ebony black hair falling out of a soft brimmed bonnet and skin darker than Tilly's own. The hair and tone hinted at a touch of gypsy blood but it was clear by the way she clutched her arm that labouring in the field was new to her.

Andrew hesitated for moment, then walked to meet her.

Tenderly, Andrew took the girl's elbow and hand in his two hands and raised her arm for a closer inspection. Tilly couldn't catch his words from that distance, but she imagined them as loving ones of comfort over the rash, familiar among the harvesters, that reddened the girl's arm and both hands.

An unwelcome flush of jealousy heated her skin more deeply than the kiss they'd just shared or even the sun overhead. She watched Andrew and the girl stand close together, his head lowered to catch her softly spoken words.

From where Tilly stood, rooted to the ground like the collapsed bines, it was as though the pair before her kissed as they had just done. The image took hold in her mind along with the words spoken by Nathaniel.

Andrew's got a girl.

Not a cruel taunt. It was true!

Tilly's throat tightened, every breath was dry and left her lungs demanding more air. Before another conscious thought could come, her feet were moving with ever increasing speed. She ignored the other workers, even those who called out to her, and ran back to the tavern, slipping through the back door.

The kitchen was mercifully empty. Judging by the sounds of voices and the occasional burst of laughter from the front, both Gwen and Agnes were needed to serve. That suited Tilly just fine.

She dredged a mug of flour and dumped it into a bowl, adding eggs and milk with the careless familiarity borne of long experience. Before long she was kneading, pulling and punching the dough, welcoming the ache of her fingers and forearms to mask to the one in her heart.

Tilly had finished enough for three loaves, leaving the dough on a shelf near the fire to prove, before she could breathe without the hitch of accompanying tears.

"I'm sure we have some, it'll be in the kitchen."

Agnes' voice, near the door that led to the bar, drew closer.

"What is it, Agnes?"

The girl started at seeing Tilly, clearly not expecting her back from her mission to the coffee palace.

"Apple cider vinegar, miss," she said, fidgeting with her apron. "Foreman says some of the workers are right red wi' hop rash."

Tilly nodded and reached for a large earthenware jug which, although sealed with a cork stopper, smelled faintly of apples as she cradled it.

When she turned back, Noah peered around the door. He smiled apologetically.

"It's first timers, of course," he explained, reaching forward to take her burden.

* * *

Twilight was falling now. In the soft blue light which was neither day nor night, Tilly accompanied Noah down to the edge of the fields where rows of tents were erected – a white canvas village on a fallow field. In the centre, a large black cauldron, almost always filled with water heated by the coals over which it sat, provided hot water for tea and bathing.

Nearby was another fire, flames of yellow and orange leaping brightly, over which a large grill – the hops devil – sat. As they approached, Tilly could smell the familiar smell of barbecued fowl. She searched among the figures returning from the fields, looking for Andrew and only half listening to Noah as he spoke.

"No matter how many times they're told, they don't cover their arms or wear the gloves. They handle the cones 'cause they've seen the others do it and they always gets themselves in strife. Some of the grown-ups have no more sense than the young ones."

There was a brief pause before he spoke again.

"It's kind of you to help out, Tilly."

At the change of inflection in Noah's voice, she turned and took in his face as they walked. In profile, she saw the boy she had known since childhood, as familiar as the Kentish landscape that was her home, and yet there was a maturity about him now that was somehow reassuring.

She waited for him to speak further, but he didn't.

They approached a tent that housed a family of six. The youngest, perhaps about four years of age, was screaming. The boy was being held by an elder sister, about twelve by Tilly's reckoning, while two other boys looked on.

Sure enough, an angry looking rash stretching from the child's forearm to elbow was the same florid hue as the screaming boy's face.

"I'll need some warm water," said Tilly.

"I'll get it." Noah said and backed out of the tent.

"Where are your mam and pa?" she asked the child's sister but the girl simply shrugged.

Tilly turned to the child's two brothers who looked at her blankly then ran outside.

She found a mug among the detritus of belongings in the tent and poured a small amount of apple cider vinegar into it. Moments later, Noah returned and ladled a portion of warm but rapidly cooling water into the mug while Tilly pulled an old kerchief from her apron pocket and dipped it in the mixture.

The child whimpered only slightly with the first touch and quietened as the long strokes of the damp cloth brought soothing relief.

Tilly fixed the twelve year old with a serious look. "Don't throw out the mug. Wash his arm again before bed time, again in the morning and whenever he complains about the pain. Do you understand?"

The girl, no more garrulous than her brothers, nodded her comprehension.

With a put-upon pout, Tilly followed Noah out into the camp, treating others for the irritation caused by the hops or too much exposure to the sun.

A smaller tent was to be their final stop. As they approached, Tilly heard two soft voices and her heart tripled its beat for a moment. She recognised *his* voice.

Tilly opened the tent flap, Noah behind her with the bucket of water. Lying on a pallet was the young woman from the afternoon and sitting beside her was Andrew. He looked up at her with surprise, but did not remove his hand from the girl's.

"You'll see, Maggie," he said, soothingly, "you'll be feeling better in no time."

Maggie. So that was her name.

Tilly swallowed and set to work.

She rubbed down the girl's arm and observed that, to be sure, the rash was severe, but it was no worse than the child she'd treated first, so surely there was no need for the woman to grimace dramatically and squeeze Andrew's hand as she did so.

She waited until the woman – *Maggie* – looked up at her, dark eyes shimmering with tears lit by the low burning lamp on a stand. Tilly gave her the same instructions she had given everyone else and stood, doing her best to avoid looking at Andrew.

Her eyes fell on a small stool, the only other piece of furniture in the tent.

On the stool sat a book with a small leather book mark peeking out between the pages. The stamped gold title on the spine shimmered in the lamplight.

Pride and Prejudice.

Andrew's got a girl.

Suddenly it all made sense. Andrew didn't just have a girl. Andrew had a *wife*.

She looked at him then, silently daring him to deny the conclusion she had drawn, a conclusion that must surely be etched on her face.

Andrew said nothing but met her gaze steadily, without apology. The scent of lemon she associated with him mingled with the smell of apple cider and so filled her throat she wondered if she could even speak.

"Noah?" she asked, her voice breathy. "It will be dark soon. Would you walk me back to the tavern?"

She could hear Noah shuffle his feet. When she turned to him, he didn't attempt to hide his surprise at Tilly requesting an escort. He blinked rapidly and nodded. "You only have to ask, Tilly."

She smiled her thanks and said no more.

Noah wasn't generally a man of many words, so the walk back to the tavern was made in silence. The sound of the harvesters, laughing and merrymaking in the field faded and gave way to the sound of chirruping crickets.

The long late summer twilight was over, the sun setting on the hopes Tilly had carried since last year, leaving her cold and numb.

How could Andrew betray her like this? She counted on him. In the darkest moments of despair since her father's death, she had clung to the memories of the September harvest and the kiss which had been so full of promise. And not just that.

She would miss reading books with Andrew, discussing the characters, debating the plots. No one else would take such an interest.

She mourned as she had mourned her father. Loss on loss. She didn't know how she could possibly bear it.

As they reached the tavern, Tilly couldn't help but take a sidelong glance at Noah in the light of the kitchen's open door. He was as tall as Andrew but more muscular and broad. He was fair haired, Andrew was dark. Andrew was educated, Noah was not.

Tilly wondered if Noah had actually ever read a book, and immediately regretted the meanness of the thought that had emerged from the bitterness in her heart.

"Tilly..." That strange inflection in his voice was back and so too the odd 'off-balance' expression he wore when they were in Andrew's tent and she had asked him to walk her home. "Can I... do you mind, if I, uh... see you?"

It was Tilly's turn to look confused.

"The tavern doesn't close until eleven. I'll be serving. You'll see me until then."

Noah's expression was now pained. "No Tilly, I want to *call* on you."

She looked at him in shock. Noah a suitor? He was more like a brother. She retreated into the tavern without a word.

Noah didn't come into the pub that night.

* * *

A week later, Tilly stepped out of the tavern craving solitude. She looked up at the sky. A deepening twilight, soft and mellow, violet in hue, settled over the village. It suited her mood.

She walked towards the stream down the laneway bordering one of the fields. Row by row, the tall forests of hops had been felled by the small army of workers. Tilly hadn't gone back to the fields after *that* evening. For the past week, she'd left the job of feeding the harvesters to Agnes, glad that long days tending both the tavern and the coffee palace occupied so much of her time.

It meant she didn't have to think. She could work herself to exhaustion and not consider Andrew who didn't want her and Noah who did.

Yet her mind wouldn't let her rest, not even when sleeping.

One night, she dreamt she walked along the river bank with Andrew, discussing a new book. They walked for miles and miles, further and further away from the village, until they had reached the wide broad road that would take them to distant London. But when she looked at her companion, it was Noah looking back at her with a patient, steady face.

In another dream, she was wed to Noah. She waited for him to come home from working in the fields but when he kissed her, it was Andrew instead.

The sound of the stream drew her closer and Tilly stepped off the lane's hard worn gravel onto the grass. She followed a path down to the water. The colours seemed deeper here. The grass along the banks was nearly emerald, the cornflowers a sapphire blue, the stream itself an inky black.

Now on her own, without so many claims on her attention, Tilly was ready to address her thoughts.

Could she have been mistaken about Andrew? For so many Septembers they had been inseparable. She loved him as she loved his passion for books, and ever since she was twelve, her years centred on his arrival in her small corner of Kent.

Of all horrid things, leave-taking is the worst.

He'd whispered those words to her when he departed, and they took on an added meaning now, when she recalled how they read them together in the edition of *Emma* that was his last parting gift.

And since the harvest dance last year – the kiss which was the start of a hundred or more dreams – she thought, she *imagined* that when they reunited at the end of this summer, it would be the beginning of a courtship.

The snap of a twig alerted Tilly to the presence of another person. Silhouetted against an indigo sky, features indistinct, was a man, his shoulders broad.

He remained silent. Tilly waited for him to identify himself, to do *something* to tell her whether to scream, converse or throw herself into his arms.

"I have tried to seek you out for a week."

The frightened pounding of Tilly's heart settled into a less frenetic beat as she recognised the voice.

"You will not look at me when I go into the tavern, you will not serve me in the coffee palace. What happened to my dear friend, the one I could always count on to discuss books?"

There was a moment's silence as she gathered her thoughts before speaking.

"*I may have lost my heart, but not my self-control.*"

Although Andrew's face was invisible in the shadows, she imagined a look of startled surprise as he realised she quoted Miss Austen back at him.

"Tilly..."

Her name, uttered with such anguish, shattered her heart completely. She waited. Waited for him to say something, anything – to tell her she was mistaken... or to tell her she was not. She needed to hear those words one way or another.

For whatever he next spoke would either bind them forever or break them apart for always.

But he said nothing. Tilly straightened abruptly, a lightning flash of anger animating her face.

"*Seldom, very seldom, does complete truth belong to any human disclosure; seldom can it happen that something is not a little disguised or a little mistaken,*" she quoted, then, "In your case, I have been mistaken."

She moved to brush past him but he grasped both her arms as she passed.

"Tilly, wait..."

"Wait? I've waited all year for you to come back! You kiss me. You make me believe there was something more in your regard for me than just a... a *fancy*. And now you're here with your *wife*."

Tilly felt the grip on her arms tighten momentarily before he released her. The rising moon cast enough light to illuminate Andrew's features. Even in the semi-darkness she could see the red heat of his anger.

"And if she were, what of it?" he said sharply. "What debt do you believe I owe you? A few fumbling kisses in the dark and you think you own me? You accuse me and then have the cheek to parade your own love-sick calf in front of..."

At the sharp crack Tilly started, surprised by the sound. Then her palm stung. She had struck him! She had no recollection of having done it. Andrew looked as startled as she did, but only for a moment before his expression cooled. He raised a hand to his cheek and rubbed it ruefully.

"I sometimes forget how young you are," he said softly, turning away from her. Then his voice hardened. "Should you be ready to discuss matters like a grown woman, you know where to find me."

He stalked off into the darkness, leaving Tilly alone with her tears.

* * *

The water pump finally yielded its treasure with a juddering groan. Tilly was vaguely aware of it splashing into the bucket as she worked the cold iron handle, arm muscles straining. She was distracted, her attention far up the road to where it disappeared between two hillocks a half mile distant.

The morning sun was warm on her back and she closed her eyes against the glaring landscape.

Today, the itinerant harvesters would be back.

She stood and reached for the bucket only to find a warm hand already on the handle.

Noah lifted it from the trough, keeping his eyes on her as he did so and yet he did not say a word, although Tilly suspected he would like to. She watched him effortlessly haul the heavy load into the kitchen as he had done every day for years, rain or shine, sleet or snow.

Never once had he drawn attention to his deed, let alone mention it. Thanks to him there was always an abundance of chopped firewood in the woodshed and the tavern roof was always in good repair. He dealt with troublemakers in the tavern with quiet authority and, every spring, helped replant the kitchen garden.

There were a hundred and one things Noah had done for her and Gwen, but never once had he spoken of love.

Only that one time had he come close to speaking of his feelings.

I want to call on you.

She had dismissed him then without a word, not intending unkindness, but with not a word of encouragement either, not when Andrew – exciting, worldly, educated Andrew – was bound to realise the error of his ways and realise she was the one who should be his wife.

Tilly shook her head. What a silly girl she had been, filled with foolish fairytale notions of love.

Last night, anticipating the return of the harvesters, she had come to realise something.

She lied to herself when she considered Noah as a brother. There was something more. To be sure, it was not the flame of youthful passion, but nonetheless it glowed steadily, like well-tended coals.

She turned back to the tavern just as the sound of laughter and songs from the first arriving workers reached her from up the road.

She didn't look back. There was no longer a yearning to search for Andrew's face. The harvest workers were now just a part of the seasons, new faces and old ebbing and flowing like the tide.

Tilly closed the door behind her, watching Noah as he finished pouring the water in to the cauldron to boil.

"There's blueberry pie for you today," she told him.

"My favourite," he replied.

"That's what you say about all my cooking."

"But I mean every word of it."

Tilly smiled. She knew he did. He stood and looked at her hesitantly. Tilly held her breath. Would he ask her to marry him? If he did, she would say yes with no regrets. She thought she could see the question on his face but he hesitated.

"Well, I'll see you at lunch then."

Tilly nodded and Noah turned away, but he paused as he reached the door.

"I brought you a gift," he said and disappeared through the door, not waiting for an acknowledgement.

Indeed, on the kitchen table was a small package wrapped in brown paper and string.

Inside was a book, a slim volume of poetry, quite unlike the practical tokens of affection that had been, she now saw, part of his unconventional courtship.

The book was inscribed in Noah's familiar handwriting, simple and precise, a verse copied from within the volume and, thus, made personal:

When you are old and grey and full of sleep, and nodding by the fire, take down this book, and slowly read, and dream of the soft look your eyes had once, and of their shadows deep. How many loved your moments of glad grace, and loved your beauty with love false or true, but one man loved the pilgrim soul in you.

THE END

ABOUT THE AUTHOR

Elizabeth Ellen Carter has won praise and a wide readership for her highly researched historical romance adventures.

The novella Nocturne was first published in 2016 for Valentine's Day.

The short story September Harvest was written for inclusion in the 2015 anthology Second Chance Cafe with authors Susanne Bellamy, Noelle Clark and Abbie Jackson.

For more information, visit eecarter.com and subscribe to her magazine Love's Great Adventure at eecarter.com/book-club

TITLES BY
ELIZABETH ELLEN CARTER

Moonstone Obsession

Moonstone Conspiracy

Warrior's Surrender

Dark Heart

Captive of the Corsairs

Revenge of the Corsairs

Shadow of the Corsairs

Nocturne

The Thief of Hearts

COMING IN 2018-2019

The King's Rogues (Four Book Series)

LEARN MORE AT EECARTER.COM
OR SEARCH
'ELIZABETH ELLEN CARTER'
ON AMAZON

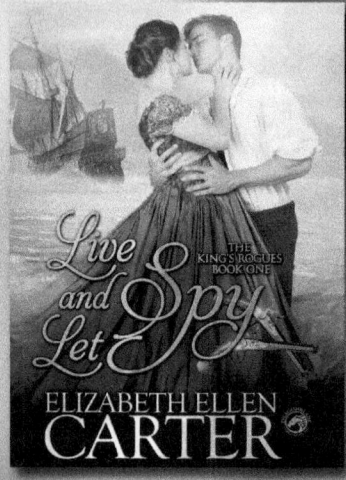

Live and Let Spy

THE KING'S ROGUES
BOOK ONE

ELIZABETH ELLEN
CARTER

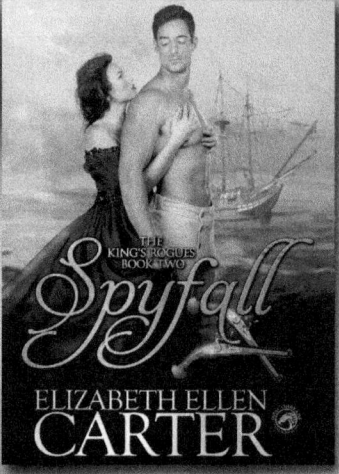

Spyfall

THE KING'S ROGUES
BOOK TWO

ELIZABETH ELLEN
CARTER

COMING 2018-2019

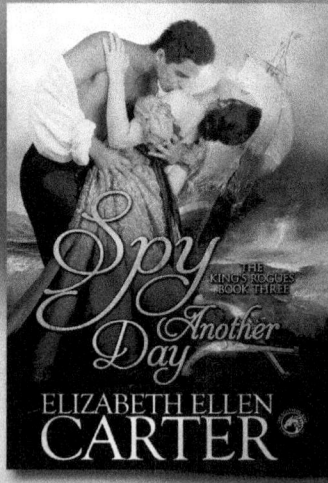

Spy Another Day

THE KING'S ROGUES
BOOK THREE

ELIZABETH ELLEN
CARTER

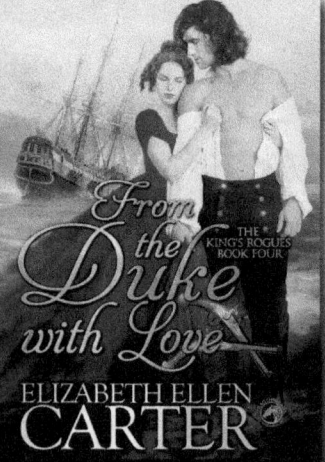

From the Duke with Love

THE KING'S ROGUES
BOOK FOUR

ELIZABETH ELLEN
CARTER

COMING FROM ELIZABETH ELLEN CARTER

ADAM HARDACRE SHOULD BE AN OFFICER IN HIS MAJESTY'S ROYAL NAVY BUT HIS LOW BIRTH CONDEMNS HIM TO THE NON-COMMISSIONED RANKS. HOWEVER, WHEN HE TRIES TO QUIT, HE'S MADE AN OFFER TOO TEMPTING TO REFUSE - CREATE A BAND OF ADVENTURERS WHO WILL SPY IN THE SERVICE OF ENGLAND AGAINST NAPOLEON.

ALL UNOFFICIALLY, OF COURSE...

THEY'RE NOT AGENTS OF THE CROWN - THEY'RE THE KING'S ROGUES.

Adam recalled his terrified sixteen-year-old self—young with no experience, but a world of opportunity ahead of him. Now he was a man with experience, but no opportunity. Well, he couldn't sit like a lumpen on this park bench until the end of time. He got to his feet.

"I hope you're not leaving on my account."

He swiftly turned. It was the civilian from the Admiralty. "No, by all means," said Adam. "Take the bench, take the park... take the devil too, for all I care. I'm leaving."

The stranger grinned, clearly amused. "I wanted to see you before I left London," he said. "And I'm much obliged to you for making it easy. I thought it would take days to find the tavern you were drowning your sorrows in."

"Who the hell do you think you are?"

The man reached into his dark blue coat and withdrew a thick white card. "I am Lord Daniel Ridgeway, and I have a proposition for you. Come to Charteris House three weeks from now." Before Adam could draw breath to refuse, Ridgeway reached back into his coat pocket and pulled out a thickish envelope. "Fifty pounds. Consider it a signing bounty."

Adam regarded the envelope. "I could walk away now and be fifty pounds the richer with no obligation to you."

"You could. But you won't."

"You seem very sure of yourself."

Ridgeway grinned again. "I know what sort of man I'm dealing with."

- from Book 1, Live And Let Spy
Coming in 2018 from Dragonblade Publishing

www.ingramcontent.com/pod-product-compliance
Lightning Source LLC
Chambersburg PA
CBHW071518100726
47908CB00004B/1217